Offering Gold Coins To A Cat

Kon Blacke

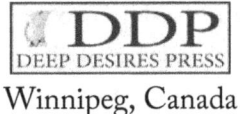

DEEP DESIRES PRESS

Winnipeg, Canada

Editor Francisco Feliciano

Published April 2023 by Deep Desires Press, an imprint of Story Perfect Inc.

Deep Desires Press
PO Box 51053 Tyndall Park
Winnipeg, Manitoba R2X 3B0
Canada

Visit http://www.deepdesirespress.com for more scorching hot erotica and erotic romance.

Subscribe to our email newsletter to get notified of all our hot new releases, sales, and giveaways! Visit deepdesirespress.com/newsletter to sign up today!

Offering Gold Coins
To A Cat

Part One

The blistering summer's day as it slunk into evening became even more sultry with thunderclouds looming, the air thick and cloying. Michael Brock loved these kinds of nights.

It meant business.

His club, *Badda-Bings*, was the biggest and best gay gentleman's club in the city as far as he was concerned, and tonight it was filled to capacity with patrons to prove it. To see all those bodies pressed together, sweating, seduction in the air as the drinks flowed, private lounges full of men doing what they desired with each other, was something to behold. Gave Michael the chills, it did.

The chill of cold, hard cash flowing into the club's coffers.

Cha-ching! Cha-ching!

To get inside *Badda-Bings* on a night like tonight was a practical impossibility. Only those men Michael fancied the look of stood a chance. And even though the queue was long as a result, snaking around the corner of the building, it didn't mean anything for the hopefuls outside.

Michael was very selective.

He had a reputation to uphold as the owner of the place, after all.

"That one, Larry—three away from where you're standing," Michael said through their communications setup to one of his bouncers while looking at the security camera's feed. "The tall boy with the cute smile and intelligent eyes; I've not seen him before."

"Him?" Larry answered, pointing immediately to the young man Michael had picked out from the rest of the hopefuls in line.

Michael smiled. Larry sure did his job brilliantly, and knowing Michael's tastes was as important to the job as the job itself, that's for sure.

"Yes him, Larry. Check his ID. If he's good, you can let him in."

"Right ya are, boss." Larry approached the young man in question. "What's ya name, buddy?" he asked, gesturing for ID at the same time.

It was handed over after a wallet was retrieved from a back pocket.

"Tachibana," the young man said softly. "My name's Tachibana Kushano—as my driver's license will no doubt tell you."

"Hey, just doin' my job. No need to get smart, buddy."

"Sorry." Tachibana lowered his gaze; Michael thought that was cute. "I didn't mean any disrespect."

Larry pressed his lips together, but brightened. "None taken." He handed back the ID, smiling knowingly. As he did so, Tachibana said, "I would like to see Michael Brock, if he's available, please."

Michael, perched within his private domain where he observed his thriving kingdom, sat up in his chair, intrigued. "Ask him why, Larry."

Larry immediately asked Tachibana, "And why do ya want to speak to Michael?"

Tachibana shrugged, his gaze turning distant. "I want to take part in *The Interview*."

Michael gasped.

Larry did too.

It was like a moment when the universe stopped, time and all.

"How does he know about that?" Michael managed, still taken aback, pleasantly so, he admitted. "Ask him how he knows, Larry. Ask him."

Larry did so.

Tachibana's reply was even more surprising. "I want my ass filled with as much cum as I can get from as many guys as possible—my boyfriend's into felching. He likes sucking it outta me once I've been wrecked. And I heard Michael was the man to speak to so that can happen."

Michael could only blink at the monitors. Larry was just as dumfounded. Because not even the regular bottom boys who frequented the club in herds over the weekends, thirsty as hell and gagging on as much cock as they could get their mouths and asses around after being bought a few drinks, were that forward.

And none of them, especially complete unknowns like Tachibana, guys Michael had never seen before either, had even heard of *The Interview*. And he didn't know Tachibana Kushano from a bar of soap.

The Interview wasn't exactly something Michael spread around for the gossiping crowds to get excited about, mostly because *The Interview* was a private and exclusive event.

So, how had Tachibana heard of it?

Normally, Michael only selected an experienced young man to participate in one of his gangbang events from those he knew personally. He was very, very selective about it. Because aside from being responsible for the bottom boy's safety, Michael had to know whether or not the guy could take it, the intensity that wasn't only about his physical state but his mental one, as well.

That's why Michael was extremely cautious— gangbangs could go wrong in a heartbeat. The result of which wouldn't be pretty if the bottom boy was pushed too far, sometimes causing a lot more than physical injuries.

He'd seen it plenty of times.

Not in his club, though.

But yeah, broken boys who weren't ready weren't a pretty sight. And Michael didn't want that to happen in his club. Not ever—the cost to his reputation could be devastating; not to mention the inevitable insurance payout that'd have to be settled out of court.

But something piqued his curiosity about the young man who'd asked for him personally, his confidence most of all. "Send him up to my office, Larry."

"Yeah, sure thing, boss."

Michael wanted...no, *needed* to talk to Tachibana before he made any decision.

My wrists still kinda hurt from yesterday, Tachibana thought, rubbing them while he was escorted towards Michael's office by one of the club's security men—a big man with pecs the size of mountains along with everything else about him. He even had a military-style buzz cut to complete the menacing look.

As anyone would, Tachibana walked in his shadow.

And as he was taken beyond the public areas, into the bowels of the club as it were, muffled dance music thumping through the walls, vibrating them, he realized he wasn't all that pleased about how he got to see Michael Brock so easily.

Now that it was happening, was this what Tachibana wanted?

Although, he didn't like how he had to lie about his boyfriend being into felching to get him this far, Riyu wouldn't do that sort of thing to him. Nope. Tachibana only served Riyu; only lived to please him.

And that was fine, because Tachibana was more than satisfied; he was dominated so completely by his boyfriend. It's how they worked together. Always had because they had an understanding which meant Riyu could ask anything of Tachibana, so long as he was loved afterwards.

They approached a door.

Tachibana sucked in a deep breath. He had to go on. Riyu wouldn't like him going back home without him having done as he'd been ordered.

I've got no choice. He smiled to himself. *But that's a good thing because Riyu makes them for me, and that's something that makes our relationship so special. I love him so much.*

"Stay here," the mountain of a man said sternly. "I'll go in first, then come get'cha. 'Kay?"

"Okay."

As the guard entered Michael Brock's office, Tachibana thought about how it didn't matter how he felt. *If Riyu wants me to get my ass wrecked by other men as punishment after I'd been lax in my duties around the house, then that's what I'll do.*

As such, Tachibana wouldn't disappoint Riyu again.

Besides, he was utterly and completely Riyu's anyways, to be used as his boyfriend saw fit. Tachibana wouldn't hesitate to do anything for Riyu either, even if that meant to his very last breath.

Michael reclined in his chair, leather creaking, fingers knitted in front of him, and putting on his best commanding look as would be expected of a man in his position.

Larry was bringing Tachibana to him, efficient and without fuss as always; he'd watched their journey on the monitor. The young man intrigued Michael. How could he not?

To his concern or perhaps it was his imagination, Michael swore he saw Tachibana rubbing his wrists. What was that all about? Was he nervous? If so…then maybe he wasn't ready for *The Interview.*

Or was it something else?

Michael dismissed that thought for a moment, pressing the intercom to gain the attention of his PA.

As Michael expected of all his staff, efficiency and politeness above all else, the response was immediate. "How can I help you, sir?"

"David, can you have the interviewers ready to go in my private room, please? Get Kaleb, Clem, Adam, and Rory for this one, alright."

"Yes, sir. Right away, sir."

As soon as Michael clicked off the intercom's outgoing button, Larry knocked on the door, his timing impeccable. "Enter."

The imposing mountain that was Larry loomed in the doorway, blocking it. With a crooked and knowing smile, he announced, "Tachibana Kushano to see ya, boss."

"Excellent." Michael sat up, realising he couldn't help himself. "Show him in, Larry, won't you?"

"Yeah, boss." Larry moved aside, gesturing for Tachibana to enter with his thick, meaty hand and sausage fingers.

What was revealed behind Larry was even more stunning than what Michael had spied through the security camera's feed. Tachibana was, and to put no finer point on it, a breath of fresh air: cool and crisp and beautiful.

Michael had to do his darndest to suppress his instant admiration.

But he also had to remain professional.

Larry left.

It was now Tachibana and Michael. Alone. Suddenly, and he didn't fully understand why, he found the air closing in around him. He shrugged it off. If there was one thing Michael never did, it was to develop any feelings towards anyone else, handsome or otherwise.

He'd been burnt too many times, by both men and women.

Clearing his throat, Michael said, "Please take a seat on the couch over there, Tachibana. And just so you know, before we proceed, I'll need to know a few things about you. Alright?"

"Sure." Tachibana nodded.

As the young man sat, thunder rumbled above the muffled din of the music from the club. There would be a storm tonight. A sign perhaps? Once more, Michael dismissed his thoughts. He had no time to think of such things.

He had questions to ask—*The Interview* already begun.

"Tell me a little bit about yourself, Tachibana."

Tachibana rubbed his chin in thought, looking up. "I'm twenty-one years old, I work in a lawyer's office as a clerk, and I like to read manga—oh, and I also love my boyfriend, Riyu."

Michael sat up even more. "And I know you've said it earlier outside when Larry asked you, but Riyu is okay with you doing this?"

"He is." A pause; a flash of something flicked across Tachibana's thoughtful and cute expression, one of his legs jiggling nervously, before he added cautiously, "He wants me to be fucked by as many guys as will have me, because it really turns him on knowing that I have been."

"And how do *you* feel about it?" Michael stood, moving closer to Tachibana, feeling the boy's intoxicating presence even more than before, like something undefinable radiated from him. He simply took Michael's breath away, breath he didn't know needed taking.

"I want it too…of course."

"I see."

Tachibana then offered a quivering smile as Michael sat next to him. Sure, he looked really nervous now, all boys in this situation were no matter how much they desired the thought of being gangbanged—or believed they desired it. Such a reaction was normal. In fact, Michael would worry more if Tachibana wasn't nervous.

"I've prepared myself," Tachibana added, looking at Michael with his green-colored wonders that were his glistening intelligence-filled eyes. "And I'll do my best to please the men you've organized for me, I promise."

Michael only offered, "And what makes you think I've organized anything?"

Tachibana was taken aback, but if Michael wasn't mistaken, looked worried too. "Please, I need this to happen."

"Then tell me why you're rubbing your wrists. You're doing it now, in fact."

Once more, surprise filled the young man's expression. "Oh, it's nothing." Tachibana seemed to blush as well, like it embarrassed him that Michael had observed such a thing. "Riyu just got a bit too enthusiastic last night in bed after he tied me up."

"Ah, you're into kink too, are you?"

Tachibana averted his eyes. "He is."

"And you?"

Without looking up, Tachibana said, "I'm into whatever he wants me to be into."

"Like being gangbanged, for example?"

"Yes, like being gangbanged." Tachibana then looked

up again, his expression clear of anything he'd worn earlier. "I'm Riyu's submissive, so I do as I'm told. Nothing wrong with that, is there?"

Michael snorted a laugh. "You're not talking to a career counsellor here—I own a club where anything goes. I've seen it all. Heck, I offer it all too. So no, there's nothing wrong with that." He studied Tachibana's reaction. None came. He therefore added, "So long as it's done right, though. With mutual consent, respect, and understanding, I mean."

Maybe that'd cause the young man to lower his guard for a moment. Reveal something, anything, which would cause Michael pause. To halt proceedings.

Michael's added words didn't give him the desired result.

Tachibana only jiggled his leg even more, an action done with even more wrist rubbing. There wasn't the whole truth being told here, Michael sensed it. Because of that, in the depths of his insides, a dark feeling, like a specter manifesting itself, came into being.

And even if Tachibana answered every question, to Michael it wasn't what was said, but what wasn't. He couldn't explain it. Perhaps he didn't want to. But it did worry him.

More than it should, really.

He then had to ask, "I need to know how you found out about me and what I do."

Tachibana shrugged. "Riyu told me about you and what you can offer here. I don't know how he knows, so don't ask, please."

He raised an eyebrow. "Fair enough."

Michael didn't know anyone by that name. Who was this Riyu character, anyway?

The boy then stood. "So…do I take off my clothes now to show you that I'm worthy of your time and that I'm ready for whatever happens next?"

That time, Michael did let his feelings show. He gulped.

While Tachibana unbuttoned his shirt he thought, *I've got to show Michael that I can do this. I know he doubts me. I don't blame him. To him, I'm a nobody…but that's how I like it. Because if I'm nothing, then I can be used however he wants me to be used.*

"You…" Michael cleared his throat. "You have a lovely slim body there, Tachibana."

"Thanks."

And then Riyu will be pleased with me for doing as I'm told.

"But…umm, you do know I won't be *involved* in the gangbang as such, don't you?"

Tachibana stopped what he was doing, thumbing the last button of his shirt. "No. I didn't know that."

Michael seemed to blush, or was it something else? Tachibana wasn't sure. "Sorry, I should have informed you earlier. I only film the action; I don't participate in it."

"Err…film?"

Michael stepped closer, grabbing Tachibana's hand. To

his further surprise, the contact held something more than a mere connection. To Tachibana, it held…comfort.

That's a…weird sensation, for sure, he mused, automatically pulling his hand away like it'd been burnt, stopping himself in time from clutching it.

Michael didn't seem bothered, which strangely put Tachibana at ease. He realized the man kind of did that to him from the moment they'd met. Although, that ease didn't transfer to the reality of being filmed while getting fucked by other men. Not really. Tachibana wasn't so sure about that.

"Seems your boyfriend didn't tell you that I'm a producer of amateur gay porn, did he?" A smile revealed, went right through Tachibana. What was that about? "And that *The Interview* is one of our most popular features of the website I upload to."

"He didn't, no."

Michael moved to hold Tachibana's hand again but stopped. "Are you sure you want to proceed, then?"

Riyu would have known I'd be filmed. It's something he'd do, not tell me everything. Then again, I didn't deserve to know. I only have to do as I am told; nothing more is expected of me.

A newfound determination came over Tachibana. "I'm sure—let's do this already, please."

"Okay. But if I sense anything's wrong at any time, I'll stop *The Interview*. Understand?"

"I do."

Michael led Tachibana to his private room down the

hallway from his office where everything was set up, including four eager guys waiting patiently for their fun, more than likely already kissing and jerking each other off.

He'd carefully chosen the men for Tachibana's first time. Men who'd give him the respect Michael knew the boy deserved, even if Tachibana didn't think so himself. After all, being shared by more than one man was intense enough, but Rory, Clem, Adam, and Kaleb would take their time, treat Tachibana right.

They'd also let Tachibana lead the proceedings, which was important.

After all, in any sexual situation, whether they believed they were being submissive or not, the bottom boy held the power, even if relinquishing control. And Michael hoped the experience to follow would reveal to Tachibana just that.

Because after talking to Tachibana, reading between the lines, even noting his body language, insecure and hesitant, Michael knew the young man believed he wasn't worthy of anything but to please others. Please his boyfriend Riyu most of all. And that's not how things worked. Not for a long-term and healthy relationship, anyway.

Therefore, by letting Tachibana participate in *The Interview*, Michael might have opened up a can of worms. Whether or not that was a good thing, time would tell. In any case, as far as he was concerned, something needed to happen.

And he would make it so…

"Are you sure you're ready?" he reiterated, about to open the door to Tachibana's debut into more than a sexual experience, but to his awakening as well…he hoped.

Michael had to admit he also loved this moment, the anticipation of what would follow. How the bottom boy would perform. How, in this case, Tachibana would.

Because, and no doubt about it, he had a feeling this gangbang scene was going to be something special.

"I said I was, so I am," Tachibana replied with a voice full of determination, and a hint of tetchiness, perhaps disguised as nerves if Michael wasn't mistaken.

Michael opened the door.

He was right, there were the four he'd organized, naked and hard and keeping each other that way, all lust-filled expressions too. It was so hot. The heat they emanated like horny animals already filled the room with its musk. Michael could taste it. He loved it.

Tachibana took a step back; Michael caught his back. "Are you alright?"

A nod, but the nerves had clearly taken him over, it seemed.

Michael had to put him at ease, break the ice. Introductions always did that. "Then in that case, Tachibana, meet Kaleb," he gestured to the closest guy, all rippling muscles. "Rory," the next man was dark-skinned and sexy as all hell. "Adam," a typical jock, cheeky smile too. "And finally, that handsome beast over there is Clem," the largest and oldest of them all was pointed out. "Guys, meet Tachibana Kushano, our newest bottom boy—so be nice. Alright?"

"Sure thing, boss," Adam said, his smile going from cheeky to carnal in a blink of an eye as Tachibana was looked up and down, feasted upon by all of them.

The others nodded their liking, salivating already, Michael knew.

Tachibana only offered a meek two-fingered wave. "Hey there, everyone. I'm here to please you all as best I can."

Clem stood; his veiny cut cock, dripping his excitement and massive, seemed to demand as much attention as the rest of him. "My, my, has an angel fallen from heaven? Because hot damn lads, we've sure got one right here as a blessing, haven't we?"

The others agreed, nice and friendly.

Tachibana *was* the center of attention.

As he should be.

"I'll set up the cameras," Michael said. "Tachibana, you can take off the rest of your clothes so the guys can see how handsome you really are."

"Sure." *I'm so nervous now; I can't believe it.* Tachibana swallowed, feeling warmth rise within him, felt himself stir. *These men are hot…such massive muscles on them. Wow. They must work out all the time. And their dicks, they're all* huge— *especially Clem's. I've never seen one that big!*

Tachibana thumbed the waistband of his jeans, readying himself to pull them down, show them all what he had. *Am I good enough for them?* He pondered that thought for a moment. *Then again, does it matter if I'm not? Their job is to fuck me, leave their jizz in my ass, and then be done with me, right? After that, I can then go home to Riyu and get my reward for being his good and obedient boy. Yes. I'll look forward to that—so let's get this over and done with.*

Tachibana dropped his jeans and underwear together.

Those in the room seemed to take in a breath, something that made Tachibana smile shyly. But he'd done it. He was ready.

"You're not an angel; you're a god, boy!" Rory said, moving so he could grab Tachibana, escort him to the massive couch where the action would soon happen. "So beautiful."

Adam, taking Tachibana's hand firmly, intertwining his fingers within Tachibana's, said, "Your first time, hey?"

Tachibana nodded, feeling himself harden even more as they began caressing him all over, something that sent delightful little shivers all through him.

Before he knew it, the men were touching him with more determination, their large warm hands everywhere. They also kissed his cheeks and ears with equally warm lips, resulting in even more shivers becoming shudders of delight.

He'd never been kissed so much before; it made him giddy.

Tachibana moaned, realising he was being taken away in the moment. It felt so good to be paid so much attention, to be wanted without the worry of what would happen afterwards. What he'd have to do because he had been pleasured as, in Tachibana's experience, nothing was given for free.

To emphasize that, Adam winked. "We'll make sure we treat you right, lovely—won't we, lads?"

There were grunts of agreement in reply, mostly through heated kisses upon Tachibana's quivering skin. Again, something he wasn't used to. Most times, Riyu got straight to business, only kissing briefly, if at all. Not that such a thing mattered—he was Riyu's submissive, so any attention was yearned for, kisses included or not.

Although Tachibana, to his surprise, and despite what he thought, noticed the rising lust in his voice, the sudden desire to do well for these handsome men, to please them as they pleased him.

He found himself saying, "Then I'll be in your care, all of you."

"You sure will be, darling," Kaleb replied, smiling, kissing Tachibana's nipple, rolling his tongue around it after that, something that caused a tingle through his rapidly rising and falling chest.

So different.

Clem then seemed to take command, as he was the one who moved into position behind Tachibana once Tachibana got onto all fours on the couch.

"Can you move your butt so I can eat you out, Tachibana?" Clem ordered with gentle authority. "I wanna get you ready for us all to have our way with you."

Tachibana did so. "Like this?" Liking how they could all see his arse properly now.

"Yeah—that's it, beautiful," Rory said, running his hand over Tachibana's cheek down to his chin.

The result of what followed next was mind-blowing.

Before Tachibana could express how it felt to have a thick masculine tongue licking his hole, over and over, wetting him, making him quiver and feel strange sensations at the base of his spine like he'd never felt before, Rory grabbed him by his jaw gently. "I heard you like kisses."

"I-I so d-do," Tachibana stuttered while Clem's tongue continued doing its thing, causing his knees to weaken, and breathe harder as he got hotter and hotter.

I'm going to be panting soon; I know it.

"Then how 'bout you open your lovely mouth for me and give me your cute tongue," Rory said. "I want to taste you, nice and deep."

Tachibana did so, amazed at how much saliva he'd produced because of his growing lust. Then, with his mouth open, lips wet, tongue dripping, he was quickly overwhelmed by both Clem and Rory's attention.

Being kissed like this is so hot while getting rimmed at the same time. I can't believe it. Oh. My. God!

Tachibana groaned deeper from his throat, really getting into it, arching his back and opening his mouth even wider for Rory, the man's tongue indeed exploring deeply. Tachibana's head spun even more, his giddiness almost out of control.

"Hey, I want a piece of that action, Rory," Adam said, coming into Tachibana's view, lust ripe in his expression.

Soon, Tachibana was dealing with two tongues...no three, one licking and readying his hole, the others vying for supremacy within his gaping, dripping mouth. Tachibana became so flushed with yearning he was glad he was naked; his skin felt like it was on fire because it was paid so much attention.

This is...amazing! Every inch of me is in a wonderland. I've...I've never felt like this before. Not ever!

His feelings became even more enhanced, when within the maelstrom of what he was already experiencing, he realized the fourth tongue, the hot wet slab of wonder belonging to Kaleb, was paying attention to his twitching dick and tightening balls.

Tachibana shuddered, stomach quivering uncontrollably, his insides trembling delightfully, right to the deepest depths of him.

I'm...not going to last long.

And to have his foreskin nibbled on, jolts of tingling joy the result, more shuddering too, was also different before it was pulled back and Tachibana's oozing with pre-cum dick was then sucked on expertly and with care.

Nope. Not long at all...

"Mhm, come and taste this pretty boy's hole, Adam," Clem said. "It's delicious."

Adam parted his kiss with a wet smack of his lips. Tachibana missed his affection already; his exploring tongue. But he didn't get long to do so. Adam was soon behind him, his tongue doing its thing, including being inserted into the quivering hole.

That *was* different!

Oh...oh, it feels...ahh...it feels so good to be fucked by something so wet and warm, not going to lie.

Adam, between his lickings, moaned, the vibrations of it coursing all through Tachibana as much as his joy. "You do taste nice. But lovely, don't be shy, come sit on my face properly." Tachibana couldn't answer. Rory was still kissing him, but he lowered his butt by opening his legs wider and arching his back more. "Yeah, that's better."

At the same time, Clem moved so his massive veiny dick, so hard and leaking and glistening, was presented to Tachibana, the reason obvious. Rory must have caught on, because he parted their kiss and did the same as Clem.

Now Tachibana had the joy of dealing with two dicks to please with his mouth instead of two tongues. What a change. One Tachibana loved the thought of, no lie.

"There, there, don't be shy, angel," Clem said, holding him under his chin to raise his face so he could slide his dick onto Tachibana's mouth proper, smiling as he did so. "You know what to do."

Tachibana nodded. "I do."

Rory added, "And I want to hear you groan and growl while you suck on our cocks, beautiful. Really let us know you're enjoying yourself."

"Yes, yes, of course."

It was then Tachibana noted how much noise Kaleb was making while he sucked, slurped, and worshipped his dick while underneath him. Such an erotic thing to hear someone enjoying themselves, that's for sure.

I know what Clem and Rory mean now, I really do.

But all too soon Adam stopped rimming, Tachibana missing his shudder-inducing attention on his wanting hole straight away. "I'm all done—I think our lovely boy is ready."

Clem said, "Looks like you enjoyed your snack before the main meal, hey, Adam?"

"I did." Adam spanked Tachibana's buttocks playfully.

But Tachibana didn't have the time or means to respond. Clem wanted to be blown, so blow him Tachibana would, with enthusiasm and thanks, no less.

As he did so, Rory encouraging him with more caresses and kisses planted just so, Tachibana moaned loudly—as he was asked to do—while he took Clem's monster of a dick into his mouth. He took in as much of it as he could, and was soon flooded with the tingling taste of Clem's salty excitement, something that washed down his throat whenever he managed to swallow, almost overwhelming him.

His taste is so strong…I love it.

Clem was just so manly, musky, and wow, his dick already filled Tachibana's mouth. He couldn't breathe. He tried and tried but couldn't get the massive dick in any further, his jaw aching and eyes watering.

"Can you take it any deeper, angel?" Clem asked, Tachibana's saliva dripping in thick strands off his chin.

"He looks so sexy looking up at you through those beautiful green tear-soaked eyes of his while his mouth is full of you, Clem," Rory said. "He's such a good boy."

Tachibana moaned even louder. His eyes were indeed filled with tears, but they were of his lust and effort, his joy because he was being complimented for what he was doing. They were also because he tried his best to do as Clem wished of him.

I'm going to take it all.

Tachibana prepared himself by taking a breath as best he could, making a long "ah" sound to open up his throat. After a moment, and spurred on by Kaleb sucking on him while Adam inserted his fingers into him to prepare Tachibana even more, he did manage to go deeper, Clem's dick touching his uvula, he was certain.

Tachibana couldn't help it.

He gagged.

With a sputter and a sharp expulsion of air, breathless and wheezing, dribbling so much saliva, tears streaming too, but loving it, Clem pulled out with a pop. "I love it when guys gag on my cock. So good. Thanks, angel."

"Hey, let me get some of that," Rory demanded lightly, chuckling. "Tachibana wants more dick in his mouth, don't you, beautiful?"

"I...d-do." More sputters and gasps, he drooled from trembling lips in thick strands.

Tachibana, even before he'd calmed, eagerly took Rory into his mouth, quivering all over with excitement, sweating, still trying to catch his breath, as well.

The man wasn't as big as Clem, but still the deed was no light task. Rory was uncut; therefore, the taste of him was stronger, more pungent. More erotic too.

If there's one thing I love, it's the taste and scent of a man's dick.

"Now for the main meal, lads," Clem said. "You first, Adam, then me and Rory, okay?"

"Right on—get ready, lovely. I'm going in!"

Tachibana grunted his consent.

Adam didn't waste any time after that.

With that all too familiar feeling pressing behind him, slowly opening his hole, stabbing pain for a moment before the rush of pleasure, Tachibana was entered.

He yelped, muffled because his mouth was still stuffed with Rory's throbbing wonder.

God! Adam's big—bigger than Riyu, that's for sure.

A deep guttural groan as both Rory and Adam gained their rhythm. Then more shudders as Tachibana tried to calm as much as he could. Remaining in control was important. He didn't want to miss any moment. Have any feeling reduced.

Because yes, being face-fucked while taken from behind at the same time was overwhelming to say the least…no, while being sucked on and being spit roasted by two eager and big men at the same time was overwhelming.

What Clem was doing, Tachibana didn't know. Then again, his scope of perception didn't extend to knowing such things, but only because Clem was probably moving around, readying himself for what he was going to do to Tachibana next.

Which was fine with Tachibana, of course.

Enough was happening already.

Rory now held Tachibana's head, gently but with determination, as he thrust and thrust into Tachibana's mouth. The noises of sucking, gulping, slurping, balls slapping against chin and backside, moans and groans, all filled the room.

All the while, Adam grappled harder onto Tachibana's hips while he obviously now gained a rhythm towards his climax.

Tachibana had to admit, he was in carnal heaven.

All this undivided attention, *all for him*, made him feel

special. He felt like he was a lot more than just a submissive to use. A fuck doll, as Riyu had called him often.

Because these men, these complete strangers, they seemed to care about him. All the while they whispered into his ear, asking how he was, if he was okay, if he liked what they did to him, if he wanted more. They always caressed him too, kissed him, even when deep inside him and otherwise busy. And being called angel, beautiful, darling, and lovely, was also nice. Hot too.

Yes, everything was amazing. Incredibly so.

Tachibana became emotional. His tears of lust and the need to do well for these men now rolled down his cheeks. But, as they did fall, he realized they were more than that. They were the tears of how he felt important. Like someone who mattered, not just someone there to abuse.

They were the tears of how he felt like he mattered.

Tachibana couldn't help himself; he began to shudder with those emotions. Cry even more.

Clem must have sensed something was up. Why wouldn't he? He'd shown he cared all along. "Are you alright, angel?"

Tachibana grunted, coming off Rory's dick for a moment, saliva dripping onto his chin again. Breathless for a moment, he managed, "I'm r-really…good, t-thanks."

"Let us know if it's too much for you, okay, beautiful?" Rory interjected.

That time Tachibana nodded, taking Rory's dick again, loving the feeling of it inside his mouth, the reaction Rory had as well.

Tachibana didn't want this to end.

No way.

But he knew it had to, inevitable, really. Mostly because Kaleb was beneath him, and had been there from the beginning, worshipping Tachibana's dick, sucking and slurping and doing his best to please.

And please Tachibana the man did.

No…I'm not going to last long. I can already feel I'm getting to the point of no return. It's tightening my insides… making me feel euphoric. I love it! Love it.

Then again, and because he was conditioned to think like that, all thanks to Riyu, he felt compelled to ask for permission to cum. He didn't though, because in the end, Tachibana realized something.

Something profound.

Yes, these handsome men got to take Tachibana how they wanted to take him. But at the same time, he was taking from them what he wanted as well.

This…this is a two-way street. Such a strange notion to even think about. Tachibana's heart fluttered. *I'm a stranger in a strange land, I really am.*

"In that case, seeing as you're all good, it's my turn to fuck you," Clem said as Tachibana felt Adam shudder and groan, collapse over him so the back of his neck was kissed and kissed. Again, so different from experience, and so good.

Adam had given Tachibana his precious load.

Three more to fill me with their love before I'm done. He liked that thought.

Adam was panting; Tachibana could hear it in his ear

before he moved, so Clem could go behind him. It didn't take long.

And like when Tachibana tried to blow him, Clem's dick almost split him down there too. "Ah, your little hole is clenching around me so tightly! It feels so good, angel. So fucking good. But relax a little, okay?"

Tachibana moaned, feeling the pain once more, longer lasting, before the pleasure visited as soon as his prostate was massaged, sending tingles all through him by Clem's actions.

Once more a rhythm was gained.

Rory pulled himself out of Tachibana's mouth, again saliva dripping off his dick and Tachibana's mouth in equal measure. Tachibana wiped his lips with the back of his hand. So much wetness, it was everywhere, all over the leather of the couch too.

He'd produced so much.

In a way, no longer sucking on Rory was both a relief— Tachibana's jaw had stopped aching—but sad as well. Tachibana wanted to taste the result of his efforts, be rewarded by them. He wanted to swallow Rory's jizz.

But he knew he couldn't.

Rory had to give it to him where Adam, and now Clem, had.

"You're so good, darling," Kaleb said coming off Tachibana's dick for a moment, for air, no doubt. "You've given me so much pre-cum, it's amazing and so, so tasty. Thank you."

He was surprised by those words. *Wow, I'm more than a*

warm dripping hole for these men, that's for sure. I'm giving to them as much as they're giving to me! And they appreciate it too!

"But I think it's time I fucked you now," Kaleb added.

"Aww, I wanted to go next," Rory said, looking hurt through Tachibana's misty tear-soaked vision.

"You'll get your turn, Rory," Clem said, grabbing Tachibana to flip him onto his back, resting him on his rippling abs and chest, where he was held tightly, lovingly.

Tachibana opened his legs, at the same time leaning back so he could kiss Clem in thanks upon his stubbled cheek; it was nice to be in a different position. "But take him like this, Kaleb. I want to see you fuck our little angel."

"I want to see him blow his load all over himself," Adam added while he moved so he could suck on Tachibana's erect nipples in turn. Something, again, that was different but sent so much delight all through Tachibana.

He also realized that being with Riyu was like being color blind, it really was, because with Clem, Rory, Adam, and Kaleb, the palette was full of color, carnal and beautiful and much needed color at that.

I've missed out on so much.

Kaleb gave Tachibana all he could moments later, shuddering, groaning, panting, face screwed up. The others cheered for him as he shot more and more of his hot, sticky jizz into Tachibana.

He smiled. *Kaleb's going to fill my guts, he really is.*

Rory then moved into position once Kaleb pulled out. Clem and Adam held Tachibana, kissed him, caressed him, did all they could to make him feel great. They succeeded. Tachibana hummed with joy; he really did.

"Cum when I cum, beautiful," Rory said with a hungry growl.

Tachibana nodded, breathing harder. "Tell me when, and I'll do my best for you."

"He's so polite, it's sexy as fuck," Adam said between licks over Tachibana's neck and chest.

Kaleb had grabbed Tachibana's dick, masturbating him gently. It felt good. Not too strong. Not too weak either. But yes, he could certainly feel himself rise to the erotic heights he needed to so he would climax.

Tachibana quivered, loving being filled, paid attention to by the others as well at the same time.

It felt so damn good.

Rory thrust and thrust, as he'd done when he face-fucked Tachibana, this time sweat dripped, though.

Clem and Adam continued their caresses.

The moment of release didn't take long for Rory or Tachibana. "Now, beautiful. Cum for me now!"

Tachibana let himself go.

He shuddered and shuddered, coming so much Clem copped a thick, sticky ribbon of it on his chin. More quivers. Gasps. Moans. More cum. So much more. Tachibana drenched himself. His whole body existed only to serve his ejaculation.

"Hell yeah!" Adam said, already licking up what Tachibana delivered.

Kaleb joined him.

I've never had anyone want to taste me before. And look at that, they all want to. They're practically wrestling with each other to get as much cum as they can, like it's a delicacy.

"You're so sweet to us by giving us so much," Clem said.

"You really are," Kaleb added, Tachibana's jizz licked from off his lips, savored, smiles all round. "You taste even better now too."

What followed was nothing short of amazing. While Tachibana cooled, clenching his anus to keep all of their cum within him as best he could, not wanting any to leak out, they kissed and kissed, holding him with such love it hurt.

Hurt in the best way.

Tachibana felt his tears again, once more for something good.

I've never felt like this before.

Clem, disturbing his reverie, said, "You'll be back soon for us, won't you, angel?"

The others stated their agreement.

Tachibana could only say, "I hope I can be, yes." And that was the truth—one which he had Michael Brock to thank for giving him such a rewarding experience.

An amazing experience that sure went both ways and meant something to us all, I've got to admit. Meant something to me too.

Michael turned off the camera, hands trembling. As he knew it would be, felt it in his gut really, what he'd filmed was one of his best scenes ever.

And it was all because of Tachibana.

The boy was a natural...no, not a natural. He was a glinting and precious jewel amongst the coal. Breathtaking. How could someone be so captivating? It was incredible watching him—his eyes were only on Tachibana the whole way through the scene.

No one else mattered.

"You...you were amazing," Michael could only say somewhat lamely after that stunning performance, still feeling the energy of the room as the guys cooled, as they embraced Tachibana who was still lying on the couch, kissing him tenderly, wandering hands and all.

They adored him.

Michael felt a little envious that they got to do those things with Tachibana. But as he turned off the lighting, packing up, that was when he noticed something was off.

Tachibana suddenly didn't look happy.

He approached, offering his hand. To his delight, Tachibana took it, the contact sending little jolts all through him. Again, that was...different.

"How do you feel after that?"

Tachibana shrugged, worry furrowing his brow. "Alright, I guess."

Michael gestured for the others to leave. "We're done here now, guys. Thanks for that—I'll see you all later."

"Anytime," Clem said, clapping his hand on Michael's back.

The others agreed.

Adam added, "Next time you need filling, Tachibana, you know who to call."

Tachibana smiled shyly. "I do, thank you."

They all kissed Tachibana in turn as they left, the boy returning the gentle gestures in kind; he really was someone special. The guys never treated anyone so well. It was nice to witness.

Touching too.

When they were left alone, Michael gave the young man his clothing back, holding them for him as he took each article in turn. He missed the sight of Tachibana's nakedness already. His natural beauty.

He said, "You seem…distracted. That's why I asked you how you felt. It's normal to feel a bit strange after you've come down from such a high. Trust me, I know."

"It's not that."

"What is it, then?"

"Why do you care?"

Michael was taken aback by such an abrupt reply. "Sorry, I didn't mean anything by it. I was just concerned about you."

After buttoning up his jeans, now slipping on his shirt, Tachibana said, "I don't mean any disrespect, because you gave me what I wanted and I appreciate it, but again, why do you care? I'm just some rando you got to film having sex for your website, aren't I? Nothing more."

Michael wanted to say Tachibana was more, so much more, but held his tongue. "You're right. I hoped you enjoyed yourself."

"I did."

"Then…I'll see you around, hey?"

Tachibana, fully dressed, headed for the door. "Yeah, you just might," he replied without turning back.

Part Two

"You're staying rather late tonight, Riyu," a warm juvenile voice said from the doorway after a light knock to gain Riyu's attention from his work.

"As are you, Jake."

The boy blushed, like full on red-cheeked as he stepped inside Riyu's office farther, tentatively so. He was adorable. "I had some work to finish up...and when I saw you were still here...I-I wanted...to see you."

"Did you, now?" Riyu raised his eyebrows. "What about?"

"I-I wanted to ask you...if you have a boyfriend."

"I don't," Riyu lied in a heavy breath. If he was reading things correctly—the body language, the nervousness, the lust which reddened Jake's face—then this cute boy who'd stayed until everyone else in the office went home to make his move, definitely wanted some action.

The kind of action that would lead to Riyu's cock being sunk deep into his mouth or ass or both, no doubt about it. The thought made Riyu harden to the point where he had to shift his weight.

He loved that he was aroused already. He also loved the game that'd follow before his lust was fulfilled.

Jake smiled in response, one which almost devastated Riyu; it was that gorgeous, so full and one that made the boy's whole face light up. Yeah, he was keen. The kid had probably been nutting for weeks as he built up the confidence to confront Riyu tonight.

That turned Riyu on even more. More so because he knew at this very moment, Tachibana was pleasing other men, fucked by them in turn, and being filmed while doing it, as well. So hot—he'd watch the video when it was uploaded, for sure. Riyu would then reward Tachibana for being his obedient boy when he got home. Reward him well with his cock sunk deeply into his ass while he begged for more from Riyu, as his submissive always did.

But not until he had his way with Jake.

Because something Riyu had never experienced before came over him as the boy sat upon his desk, seductively running his delicate fingers over Riyu's chest, grabbing his tie, making him tingle all over, and that was the sudden desire he had for someone other than Tachibana.

This blond-haired boy before him, freckles and button nose, innocent smile and devilish eyes, so cute, was a treasure.

One Riyu wanted…no, needed to discover.

Riyu, feeling his libido rise even more as all his erotic thoughts swarmed around his head, had to ask, "How old are you again, Jake?"

Not that the answer mattered.

Riyu would have him.

A momentary look of surprise resulted, dissipating the lust, the electricity, that'd been built in such a short a time between them. "Err…I'm e-eighteen—why?"

"Nothing," Riyu pressed his lips together, "just making sure."

He knew Jake was lying; knew the boy's true age. He wasn't turning eighteen until next month. Riyu had checked his personnel file a week or so ago after the boy began taking an interest, sniffing around him more and more like a little puppy craving attention, complete with shy glances at the photocopier, the brushing of hands at the water cooler, and the reserved seat at the cafeteria during breaks so Riyu could always sit next to him.

Again, Jake was just so cute in every way.

Such a turn on.

So, for now, Riyu let Jake continue touching him, really enjoying the tentative seduction he attempted, something that re-energized their connection, for sure.

And yeah, Riyu would soon turn things to how he liked it. He'd soon dominate Jake. Really show him how men pleasured those who wanted it, who were panting for it, as Jake was now.

With clear nerves shaking his voice, Jake asked, "I h-heard you liked...boys."

"You heard that, did you?"

"I did." A nod. "And...and I like b-boys too."

Riyu now smiled, placing a hand onto Jake's knee. "Are you ready for what's going to happen next, though?"

"I am." A little moan from Jake at the contact too. Again, so cute. "So, tell me what I-I can do for you to be your g-good boy, Riyu. Tell me *please*. I want to d-do my best...for you."

"I know you'll do your best; I'll make sure of it."

As quick as a flash, and with Jake's words all the permission Riyu required, he grabbed the boy, pushing him onto the desk proper so he was flat on his back, crashing a hungry kiss onto his sweet, sweet lips moments later.

Jake opened his mouth to Riyu.

Riyu liked that he did already. There's nothing better than a boy giving himself over to him completely. That's why he liked Tachibana. And that's why Riyu knew he'd like Jake too.

Jake moaned with more intent as Riyu dominated him, tongues rolling, dancing, as they ground their bodies, chest against chest, groin against groin. The air was thick with their lust and determination. Riyu was as hard as ever—Jake was too, from what he could feel.

This was so fucking hot.

Riyu parted their contact, lips tingling, already feeling flushed with his erotic intentions. Intentions he would follow through with, not caring he was cheating on Tachibana with an underage boy.

He stared into Jake's beautiful autumn-brown eyes for a moment, grabbing him tighter, trembling with lust, before he ordered, "Get your fucking clothes off, boy. Give yourself to me, utterly and completely. Now!"

"Yes, Riyu!" Jake replied straight away, flushed, panting, but clearly understanding that Riyu's words were an order that he had to reply properly to—which he had.

"That's a good boy."

Riyu gave the boy a moment to do as he requested. But

as Jake began unbuttoning his shirt, something struck his expression which worried Riyu.

"Do you...have any c-condoms here?" the boy asked timidly.

Riyu didn't do protection—it restricted things too much. He much preferred the skin on skin feel, the rawness of barebacking. "No, I don't. But what does it matter, anyway?"

Jake sat up looking upset all of a sudden, eyes wide. "It matters a lot, actually."

Riyu shrugged. "I'll pull out before I ejaculate. No biggie."

"It is a..." Jake's expression of concern didn't change. He then tried to clamber away from underneath Riyu, pushing him so he could do so. "It is a big deal. I can't—"

"Wait a minute!" Riyu saw red. He grabbed the boy by his shoulders, as hard as he could grip; Jake winced. "You came into my office to seduce me, then when you get me all revved up and as horny as hell for you, you promising you'll be my good boy, you now want to back out?"

A quick look away. "Yeah...I do."

"Fuck off, you do. You'll give yourself to me, as you wanted it. Got me?"

Jake, returning his attention, gasped. He then pushed Riyu away with greater intent, a desperate one, really. But his expression had turned to one of fear. "Please, Riyu. I didn't mean to tease you, honest. I just want...I've changed my mind. I can't do this with you right now."

"What the...? I don't think so, you little fuck." Riyu

shoved Jake onto the desk, harder than before. Jake let out an *oof* as his back struck the wood. "Fucking get your clothes off and open your legs for me. Then I might forgive you for what you've done, you fucking little cockteaser."

That was when Jake struck Riyu across the cheek. *Slap!* The sting was unbelievable, sending him into a spin, stars scintillating before his eyes.

His whole face ached.

When he'd gathered himself, a moment that took longer than he'd hoped, his cock still hard—he liked it a bit rough—unfortunately, Jake was gone.

"You dirty fucker!" Riyu shouted to his now empty office, unzipping to grab his raging boner, tugging on it until he angrily spurted his hot jizz all over his fake oak wooden desk in thick ribbons, quivering and panting, moments later.

He didn't feel any better for it.

Sweat dripped off his nose after he'd cum, annoying him further. He wanted Jake. Wanted to own him. "You're gonna fucking pay for this when I get a hold'a you, Jake!" he shouted into the void. "I'm also going to fucking kill you! You hear me, Jake? Imma gonna kill you!"

Riyu, once calm enough, had a further thought. He smiled wickedly, thinking about how it might have been Jake who'd turned him on, but it would be someone else who'd pay for what had happened.

"No!" he yelled. "It's gonna be Tachibana who won't know what hit him now, 'cause he's gonna get punished for this, big time. And yes, it's all your fault, Jake! I hope you *can* hear me, you dirty little cockteaser. I hope you can hear me! This is all your fault!"

Tachibana, sore and exhausted from his ordeal, yet happy as a clam though, managed to get home without too much bother. *That Michael sure is acting kinda weird, though. Why's he getting all concerned about me? He got what he wanted. He'd filmed me getting fucked. That's the end of it. Right?*

He pulled into his building's carpark.

Then again...I felt something. I felt something when he touched me. When he gave me my clothing. And it was more...profound than when Clem and the others touched me. What's that about?

After riding the elevator to the fourth floor, he opened his front door with his key card and security code, stepping inside, liking how he was home and amongst familiar things.

"Tachibana! Get in here!" Riyu shouted from beyond the hallway.

His boyfriend's stern voice shocked him. What had happened? He'd done as he was asked. Surely, he was now his good boy.

Wasn't he?

Tachibana went to Riyu, concern flushing through him. "What's the matter, Riyu?"

Riyu looked pissed, all red-faced and glaring eyes as he stood from his favorite chair, the one with the best view of the TV. Most times Tachibana wasn't allowed to sit on the couches anyway, his place was by Riyu's feet.

With is voice rough and lust-filled, he demanded, "Get your fucking clothes off and bend over, facing away from me. And for fuck's sake, don't speak anymore. Don't complain like you always do, either. Just do it. I'm not in the fucking mood for your shit tonight."

Tachibana became confused. He never complained. He always did what Riyu asked of him without question. Even when he was told he had to eat out of a bowl on the floor next to Riyu's dining room chair that one time after not having dinner prepared on time.

He got naked within moments.

Tachibana knew that when Riyu was like this, probably frustrated about something, angry too, it was best to not offer anything other than complete obedience. Just take whatever was coming to him.

Riyu, producing a flexible bamboo cane, from where Tachibana couldn't guess, said, "Turn around. I'm gonna fucking whip your ass red raw so you won't be able to sit for a week. Then I'm gonna fuck you for being such a dirty little slut tonight."

Tachibana's stomach turned, but not in a good way, as he once more did as he was told. Riyu never hit him. Sure, he was often tied up, blindfolded sometimes. But hit?

What had happened today to make Riyu do this?

Riyu snorted derisively. "Gah! I can see cum dribbling outta your filthy fucked arse. You're so fucking disgusting it makes me sick, Tachibana. Now get ready, I'm gonna give you what you truly deserve."

Tachibana didn't reply. He knew he couldn't—the outcome of what followed would be worse if he did.

What Tachibana experienced after that he wouldn't have expected in a million years. Being caned in such a way, with no explanation, no reason, wasn't enjoyable. Each hit that struck his bare buttocks stung unbelievably. Made him lose his breath, hiss through his teeth from the pain. Shock him to his core. He had to try as best he could to stop from yelping, often failing.

Which made Riyu even angrier.

Tachibana hurt, and not just where he was hit. Something had changed within Riyu. But the stinging he felt with each strike made him shudder in agony more and more. He didn't get the chance to contemplate the reasons. His head was muddled, as much as his body was in agony.

Swish, whack!

Swish, whack!

Riyu didn't stop; he was like a man possessed. In such a state, Tachibana realized there wasn't anything he could do, could have done, to prevent this.

Swish, whack!

Swish, whack!

Swish, whack!

"Fucking take this, slut!" Riyu almost roared.

Riyu struck Tachibana's buttocks over and over again. The sting, the pain, the leg wobbling agony, gaining more and more in strength as he was hit and hit, became too much.

Tears flowed, but for a different reason than earlier. This time, they were from…disappointment. What Tachibana expected was to be loved. Rewarded for doing as he was told. The reality, as his tears dripped rhythmically onto the wooden coffee table between his hands, was far, far different. He was being punished in the worst way imaginable.

What for? He didn't know.

Tachibana soon collapsed under the weight of his pain, overwhelmed beyond words. Beyond anything he'd ever felt. He was sure he was bleeding, for he felt more than Clem, Adam's, Rory's, and Kaleb's jizz trickle from himself.

He began to cry in earnest.

"Get up!" Riyu screamed. "Get up, Tachibana! I'm not finished yet!"

"Yes...s-sir."

He struggled but got back onto all fours for Riyu. He had to. If he didn't, the resulting punishment could be even worse. Not that he could imagine such a thing, this was by far the worst Riyu had done to him.

What did I do to deserve this?

"I'm not satisfied yet, so how about proving to me what a filthy faggot you are, and open your legs for me, huh?"

Tachibana obeyed, crying so that his whole body quivered uncontrollably. He wanted this to stop. He didn't deserve such treatment.

Not at all.

And just when he thought he could take no more, unable to get back up if he collapsed again, Riyu fucked him like he was nothing. Worse than nothing, because there was no emotion connected to it like every other time, only anger.

No, not anger...loathing.

Tachibana *was* less than nothing to Riyu, it seemed.

Worse than that, he was a whipping dog now. Tachibana hated what he'd become because of Riyu.

Hated it to his soul.

When Riyu came inside him, a little grunt indicating he had, which thankfully didn't take very long, Riyu pulled out and left Tachibana alone. No comfort. No love.

Why?

He collapsed again, now a mess on the coffee table after experiencing the horror that had become such a disturbing reality since arriving home.

Tachibana cried and cried, hot tears soaking his face, unable to move.

After an eternity, one where Tachibana dared not move for the fear of provoking Riyu further, he heard, "Get to fucking bed—I don't want to see you anymore."

What? He doesn't want to see me anymore?

Those words had stung even more than the cane had.

Tachibana struggled to his feet, wobbling, still feeling the pain of being caned over and over again for no reason, then fucked for good measure. He went to his bedroom, realising he hadn't eaten. His stomach growled. He hadn't been told he could eat.

Again, all part of his punishment, no doubt. For what though, perhaps he'd never find out.

But as he slipped between the sheets, gingerly so with his blood staining them, all thanks to Riyu's temper for no reason he could fathom, pain still searing making him hiss through his teeth whenever he moved, Tachibana realized one thing.

Riyu is different. He's not the same as before. Is this all my fault? He shook his head, cradling into the foetal position while he wept softly to himself.

That night, Riyu didn't join him.

A good thing, I suppose, Tachibana considered as he thought about something he would have never believed he would.

He thought about Michael Brock, also Clem, Rory, Kaleb, and Adam, but mostly Michael. The way he touched him; a caring, almost loving touch that sent sparks of pleasure all through Tachibana.

Is it wrong to want to be with someone other than Riyu? Someone who would perhaps want me for being me? Someone who cares for me enough to provide me with something I now desire above all else. Love.

As he thought about it further, that's when Tachibana realized, as if it were a bolt from the heavens, Michael had given him something special. He'd given him the gift of what it would feel like to be respected and treated as an equal. The men chosen for him done deliberately so.

Did Michael *really* care for him, then?

Then again, why would anyone care for me, let alone want me? I'm nothing, not even worthy of being someone's whipping dog, am I? Normally Riyu would at least comfort me after punishment. Not tonight. I'm truly nothing to him. More likely nothing to anyone else either.

That's when he knew—what he had with Riyu, the good times they'd shared, enjoying being his submissive, the mutual respect they once had— it was all over.

Truly over.

Tachibana had no idea what would happen to him now.

Eventually, and with the wind and thunder of the storm raging outside, lightning flashing between the gaps in the curtains, feeling exhausted, it was his tears that eventually sent him into a restless sleep.

There was a sharp knock upon Michael's door, startling him from his study.

"Who the hell is it calling at this hour?" He glanced at the desk's clock. It was 7.30am. His PA David hadn't arrived yet—last night's storm had downed trees, traffic in chaos as a result.

"It's…it's me, Dad."

Michael sighed. "Before you even come in, how much do you want this time—just tell me through the door. Save us both time."

"I don't want any money."

Michael was shocked. "That'll be a bloody first. Usually, it's you calling so that I open my wallet for either you or for that blood-sucking woman you call your mother."

No reply.

That's when Michael knew something was up. Normally he and Jake argued, fought like cats and dogs, really. Which Michael hated. It wasn't the boy's fault he was born to two people who meant nothing to each other than a fling one drunken night. Wasn't his fault he looked so much like her either. Because, goddamn-it, the boy reminded Michael of his mistake every day. It hurt so much. It honestly did.

With a deep sigh, expecting the worst, but realising it

would probably be more than that, Michael said, "Come in then, Jake."

Jake entered; head hung low, shoulders slumped. "Sorry, Dad."

"What are you apologising for?"

"I've done a terrible thing."

Again shock. "Okay. Then I think you'd better sit down and tell me everything, seeing as you've made the effort to come here and talk to me."

"Sure." Jake quickly sat on the large couch that dominated Michael's office—his interview couch. The one Tachibana had sat upon only last night.

Michael joined him. "What's this about?"

Jake sucked in a breath, heaving it, really. "I let my jealousy ruin a relationship, Dad."

Michael remained in a constant state of surprise by what he was told, surprising in itself. "Why have you come to me?"

"Because Mum wouldn't understand."

"Why not?"

"Because I fancied a guy and I got jealous that his boyfriend had him and I didn't, that's why—you know what she's like, thanks to you."

"You're *gay*?"

A look of annoyance shot at him. "This is what you're focusing on, Dad?"

Michael had to take some time to process everything so far. "I mean...yeah. I need to understand you if I'm going to help you, Jake. It's not like we talk often, is it?"

Jake nodded. "True that." He shifted his weight. "I'm

gay, Dad. There. Now you know officially, as if it would make a difference, anyway. Happy?"

Michael ignored the intended barbs full of venom. "I am. Thanks."

But despite his standoffish attempt, unbelievably he found himself hugging his son. A gesture, after a while, that was thankfully returned. They had a moment, they really did.

Their first.

He added, "So, how about you tell me from the beginning what happened now that we've made some progress here."

Another deep intake of air. "I'm hot for this guy named Riyu…and I know he had a boyfriend—"

Something fell into place for Michael. "Tachibana Kushano."

A snort. "I know that you know Tachibana—I'm getting to that, if you let me finish."

"Fair enough."

Jake shifted his weight again, leather creaking. "I told Riyu about what you do here with all the pretty guys. Guys like Tachibana. And I knew you wouldn't say no to him either. It was all part of my plan to get to Riyu without Tachibana interfering."

Michael felt a creeping dread crawl through him. "What did you do?"

Jake went red. "I went too far."

"What do you mean, you went too far?"

"I intended…I went into Riyu's office last night knowing he'd be in there alone after he'd sent Tachibana to you. We all work together. I...I then tried to seduce him, Dad. I tried to get him to have me behind his boyfriend's back."

Michael took in a sharp breath, again in surprise. "Aside from the fact you're only seventeen, what were you thinking?" he blurted.

Sudden anger in Jake's eyes resulted along with that reddening face of his. "I was thinking like you," was the acidic retort. "Thinking with my dick, like how you thought with it when it came to my mum, didn't you?" There was then hurt in his eyes, clearly the past was still an open wound for him. For Michael as well, after hearing those words.

But Jake wasn't finished, far from it. "About how you fucked her because she was your little experiment into hetero sex; just as Riyu, to my shame I now realize, was my experiment to see how far I could go to get what I wanted."

That hurt. His words. The way Jake said them. Everything. Michael sat for a moment in silence. Dumbfounded. Guilty. But above all, angry at himself for everything he hadn't done for his son up until now. Because how could Jake understand what had happened between him and his mother? He couldn't.

Heck, Michael didn't even understand it himself.

All he could manage after a moment was a whispered and rather lame, "I'm sorry. Please...go on."

Tears rolled down Jake's cheeks to drip off his chin. "I'm sorry too."

Another embrace. That one, if Michael wasn't mistaken, was the first they'd achieved to begin a healing process that was long overdue between them. Sure, it wouldn't close the wounds, far from it, but a step was a step. And this had been the biggest one of them all.

"Go on," was all he prompted, also wiping his eyes of emotions.

"Riyu...he tried to force himself on me when I got a bit too...eager."

"What?" Again, surprise, now mixed with anger and everything else within him, including concern, rose up to almost make him choke.

Michael had to calm himself, mentally tell himself over and over, otherwise they'd get nowhere here. He didn't want that.

Jake's bottom lip trembled. "He...he only came onto me after I...kinda led him on. But even after I said no to him after I realized what I was doing, what a dick I'd been, he still tried to...he didn't stop, Dad."

Michael's world, his whole office, spun. He felt nauseous. "Did he? You know...*rape you?*"

Jake shook his head slowly. "He didn't...I said no when things got too heated. But...but I had to hit him to stop him, he was that worked up because of what I'd done. Otherwise, I knew he would have."

More tears.

Another long moment passed, again one punctuated with an embrace. What else could Michael do? He'd never been in this position before. And as he knew, right to his gut, the reason for Jake's visit was indeed something he could have never guessed.

But it also added pieces to the puzzle.

Michael kissed Jake's forehead. "It's not your fault. If you said no, even after initiating something, it's still no. I'm glad you were able to defend yourself. That the worst didn't happen."

"I know…but he got mad, Dad. Real mad. I heard him say he's going to punish Tachibana for what I did to him. So you're wrong, this is all my fault."

That wasn't a surprise for a change, considering how Tachibana had acted. How the whole 'being a submissive' thing didn't quite gel with Michael, because to him it sounded like a toxic relationship in disguise. He should know. He had one of those with Jake's mother.

He asked, "Riyu said that?"

"He did—and that's the terrible thing I did, Dad. So yeah, because I acted like a horny bottom boy, just like the ones you get in here all the time, I made things worse. I should have known Riyu is someone who likes to treat others like he owns them, because that's how he looked at me last night. Like he wanted to own me."

"It's *not* your fault; get that in your head."

"But…but because of me, it's Tachibana who's going to suffer. Riyu was fuming, Dad. He really was. He even said he wanted to kill me!"

"What!" Michael hadn't thought of that—because when a controller loses control, doesn't get what he wants, that's when things turned ugly.

Really ugly.

He got up, rushing to his desk and stabbing the intercom's outgoing button seconds later. "David! Are you there, David?"

"Yes, sir."

"Get Larry in here…now!"

"Right away, sir."

Part Three

Tachibana woke with pain.

To make matters worse, his tears were still fresh, stinging his eyes. He'd cried most of the night. Struggled with what had happened most of all. In truth, he'd been scarred so deeply, and not just physically, the wounds would remain with him for the rest of his life.

What did I... What did I do...? What did I do wrong? He replayed events over and over in his mind, unable to make any sense of it.

None at all.

He gingerly got out of bed, heading for the shower, not that anything would wash away the stain of what Riyu had done to him.

He hit me...again and again. He hit me like he enjoyed it. He's never done that before, even when he got aggressively dominant sometimes and tied me up, gagged and blindfolded me, before fucking me. What did I do wrong? He...hit me.

It may be a new day, but Tachibana's hopes of things being any better between him and Riyu, damage done, taken its toll, were slim to none.

I can't go on from here. Not with him. Not after he treated me like that.

In fact, Tachibana held no hope at all.

It's over.

The shower's warm water didn't help. No surprise there. When dried and dressed, still careful not to touch the burning pain stinging his buttocks, his underwear touching the tender skin there almost too much to bear if he moved wrong, Tachibana went into the kitchen to fix himself breakfast.

He ate standing up.

It was then Tachibana realized he hadn't eaten since lunchtime yesterday. But because of how he felt, depressed really, he forced himself to eat something, managing half a bowl of cornflakes and a cup of coffee before giving up.

He also realized Riyu wasn't home.

Riyu probably went to work early, not wanting to see me. Good. I don't want to see him either.

There was a loud knock on the door, startling him.

"Who could that be?"

Tachibana checked the time on the wall clock. It was just after 10.00am; he had the day off from work because of all the extra shifts he'd been pulling to meet a deadline. A blessing in disguise that he had, really. It meant he wouldn't have to see Riyu. They did work together, after all.

That's how they'd met.

The person on the other side of the door impatiently knocked again. As he made his way to the front door, telling them he was coming, Tachibana's thoughts wandered to that day when Riyu came into his life.

It was early on a Monday morning, the caffeine hit from the two coffees Tachibana had drunk were still trying to take effect—it'd been a heavy weekend of partying. One guy he'd locked lips with last night, he was kind of interested in. Cute too.

Tachibana gave him a blowjob in the understairs' cupboard of the house they'd found themselves at.

Tachibana couldn't remember his name.

In the end though, what he did remember was that the guy was too needy. Always fawning over Tachibana, especially after he'd swallowed. So lame. Why couldn't he meet someone who took command? Someone who knew what they wanted so Tachibana could give it to them without any fuss?

A clearing of a throat disturbed him.

Tachibana looked up from his blazing computer screen displaying the account's file he was working on. "Good morning, Mister Anderson," he greeted his department's head, a slight bow added.

"Good morning, Mister Kushano," Mister Anderson replied with equal professionalism. Always professional. "I'd like you to meet our newest employee, and someone who'll be working closely with you." He stepped aside. "May I present Mister Goya, Riyu Goya—Riyu, this is Tachibana Kushano."

The man named Riyu wasn't anything special. Not at first glance. He had black hair, kind of greasy really, average height, medium build. But what struck Tachibana the most about him wasn't his physical appearances. No. They were his eyes, dark smouldering eyes that pierced him to his soul, demanding attention.

Demanding obedience.

Tachibana was smitten already.

The handshake reinforced his feelings; it held strength within it. A strength Tachibana hadn't felt before from any other guy. By that time, Mister Anderson had left, no doubt to greet the rest of his staff or ogle over the ladies working in reception.

Tachibana was left alone with Riyu.

The air became thick between them; he had to concentrate just to breathe; such a strange, but intoxicating, feeling. Wonderful.

Straight off the bat, Riyu, pulling Tachibana closer, so close he could feel his breath against his neck, so erotic, whispered, "I want to dominate you, as I know you want me to when I have my way with you."

Riyu's hand squeezed tighter within Tachibana's.

Tachibana's heart raced, making him feel giddy. "Then... then do so."

"Good. But just know; I'll never hurt you without comforting you afterwards. Not ever. You can trust me on that."

Tachibana gulped but nodded. "Then I'm yours, Riyu."

Back in the moment, he uttered, "So much for his promise of not hurting me without comfort." *And I'm going to have to ask Mister Anderson to change departments after the weekend. That's all I need!*

Tachibana sighed sadly.

His life had changed dramatically in twenty-four hours. Yes, he'd agreed to the gangbang Riyu insisted he attend after being punished for not doing his household duties, to his mistake he now realized, but that wasn't the worst of it.

Because when he thought about it more deeply, Riyu had set him up for failure. That fateful night he hadn't made dinner on time or cleaned up, was one of the evenings he had to stay back and work.

That deadline Mister Anderson had set loomed.

Still, despite the unfairness of it, Tachibana accepted in the hope Riyu would be pleased with him, call him his good boy and make love to him afterwards. Like he usually did. What was submission without the comfort afterwards?

Unfortunately, there was no comfort any longer. Tachibana's punishment continued to its frightening conclusion. The reason unknown. And it was a punishment he wouldn't have even begun to imagine. He still found it hard to believe.

His body believed it, though; the medicinal cream he'd applied to the terrible angry red lines marring his buttocks not doing much to ease the discomfort.

Not at all.

Tachibana opened the front door. Greeting him was the one man he didn't expect standing there, looming like the mountain he was to block the view beyond.

"Larry!"

"Ya okay, buddy?" was all that was offered, no hello or anything—the man got straight to business.

Tachibana shrugged. "Depends on what you mean by that, doesn't it?"

Larry's eyes narrowed. "What did he do to ya?"

Tachibana took a step back. "How do—?"

"I know 'cause it's my job to know." The man cracked his knuckles. "Now, where is he? The little fuck is gonna get ten-fold back what he's done to ya."

Tachibana's head spun. "He's…Riyu's not here—he must be at work."

"Then let's go find the asshole." Larry turned, heading down the corridor towards the elevator. "Comin'?"

Tachibana closed the front door. "Looks like I am, doesn't it?"

"It does."

Outside the apartment, heading towards Larry's sleek black car parked in the street in front of the building, the man casting his shadow over Tachibana like a blanket, the petrichor and ozone smells after last night's storm greeted Tachibana. The skies were blue to forever now, even if there was debris, leaves, and broken branches off trees strewn everywhere.

"Where's the office he works at?" Larry almost demanded.

"It's on Collins Street, opposite the Athenaeum Theater," he replied, rising nervousness making itself known.

He didn't want to see Riyu...not even with Larry by his side.

Larry opened the back door to his car. "Get in."

"But I..."

"I said get in." Larry's expression softened. "Please."

Tachibana obeyed. *I always do as I'm told, don't I? Fat lot of good it did me, though. I no longer have a boyfriend. And the apartment belongs to Riyu, so I no longer have a place to stay either. What am I going to do now?*

After gingerly trying to get comfortable sitting down, failing really, achieving a sort of sideways sit to avoid any discomfort, thankfully the drive to work didn't take long. A relief. Tachibana was grateful he had the foresight to bring the medicinal cream with him, the tube snug in his front pocket.

As the car was pulled into a parking bay, Tachibana had to ask, "How do you know what happened last night?" But the question was the first of many.

So many.

Larry, looking at Tachibana via the rear vision mirror stated, "Jake told us everythin'."

He was taken aback. "Jake?"

"Yeah, Jake."

And that seemed to be the end of things, not that it cleared anything up. What did the office gofer boy have to do with all this? Why was Larry involved? And what would Larry do when they found Riyu?

Tachibana gulped.

Before he could ask any of the other questions spinning around his head like random flotsam caught within a whirlpool, confusion still reigning, Larry added, "Just to fill in the blank for ya, 'cause I can see you're a little confused; even though Jake has taken on his mother's maiden name for his surname, he's Michael Brock's son."

"He is?" But despite being colored surprised, Tachibana believed he understood, that pieces began to fall into place. "Jake is Michael's son?"

"That's what I said, buddy." Larry undid his seatbelt. "And it was Jake who told Riyu to send you to Michael yesterday 'cause he wanted you outta the way."

"Wait..." Then even more pieces clicked together, slowly, one by one. Terribly so. "Jake? Jake...wanted me out of the way?"

"He did—and I don't think I need to tell ya why, do I?"

So that's what changed with Riyu. Why he acted like he did. He was…he wanted Jake after the boy made it clear he was interested in him.

Tachibana saw red, clenching his fists, knuckles whitening.

He'd been treated in the most horrible way, dumped really, all because an underage boy took a fancy to Riyu…and Riyu did what? Went for it hook, line, and sinker! Tachibana shivered, like someone had just walked over his grave. Riyu was a pervert, in more ways than one, he realized.

But the puzzle was completed.

Tachibana became angry. "What the hell!" he blurted, suddenly embarrassed he'd done so when Larry glanced at him proper, smiling knowingly.

"I'd be upset too."

"Sorry." He hung his head.

"Yeah, no worries, but just so you've got all the info, Riyu tried to rape Jake last night—thankfully, the kid had the smarts to stop him in time. That or he got lucky. Very lucky."

"I'm…not surprised." And that time Tachibana wasn't. "When Riyu gets a hold of someone who interests him, he doesn't let go. I should know. From the first time he saw me, he made me his." He sighed, suddenly feeling sorry for Jake, even though he was the cause of what had happened, his anger ebbing away. "The boy doesn't know about the monster he's woken, does he?"

"You're right, he doesn't." Larry got out of the car, soon

opening the passenger door for Tachibana. "Jake overheard Riyu say he was gonna get him back for what he'd done; the kid's scared outta his mind. He also heard that Riyu will punish ya for what happened as well."

Tachibana felt his heart sink, the soreness he felt made all the more prevalent. "He *did* punish me."

Larry gently placed his hand onto Tachibana's shoulder. "What did he do to ya? Tell me, buddy."

"I'll only say I'm constantly being reminded of the fact I'm no longer someone Riyu's interested in, and leave it at that."

Larry pressed his lips together, concern etched upon his craggy features. "Riyu won't hurt ya no more. Not Jake either. As my word is my honor, I'll protect ya both."

"Is that a promise?"

Larry snorted a laugh. "It sure fuckin' is."

"I want to believe you." But as far as Tachibana was concerned, the damage was done.

Nothing more Riyu could do could hurt him. *I can't help worry about Jake though, despite what he did. Then again, perhaps the boy did me a favor. He certainly revealed Riyu's true nature, opened my eyes, didn't he?*

Jake hadn't been right all morning: nervous, on edge, stomach tight. He even bit his nails, so much so one or two now hurt. He was so stressed, couldn't eat, paced a lot; got into trouble even more than usual with Mister Anderson and all the other department workers for being distracted too. He couldn't help it.

Sure, talking with his dad earlier had helped a little.

But even that heart-to-heart between zebras couldn't stop the lion prowling the savannah, could it? Couldn't stop Riyu, even with Larry looking out for him. The giant man couldn't be everywhere; couldn't be at work with him... Could he?

And what made Jake's nerves even more shredded was the fact Riyu wasn't in the office this morning. He hadn't called in sick either. Where was he? It was almost like the calm before the storm.

Jake didn't like that feeling.

To be honest, he was at his wits end about what would happen to him now that he'd stirred up Riyu's wrath because he acted without thinking, letting his dick control his actions.

"I'm such an idiot," he whispered to himself.

And what's more, Tachibana had been punished because of what he'd done. Or rather, what he *hadn't* done because he realized his mistake in time—foolishly wanting to lose his virginity to Riyu.

"Poor Tachibana," he whispered to himself while the printer ran off hard copies of the files legally required to be done as such. "Why did I have to go into his office last night? Why?"

Before Jake could quantify his reasons, the door to the photocopy room banged open, making him jump out of his skin. He turned, gasping, heart lodged in his throat. It was Judy, the office's resident gossip, and his friend.

She placed one hand onto her hip, studying Jake.

"What's up your jacksie this morning, Jake-y boy? Ya look like ya seen a ghost."

Jake sucked in a breath after his heart dislodged from his throat and he'd calmed a little. "Err…nothing."

"Sure don't look like nothin' ta me." She was chewing gum, the sound of it grating already as she rolled it around her mouth while she talked. "Ya seem more nervous than a rattlesnake at a rocking chair convention, don't ya."

"If you say so." Jake grabbed the paperwork he needed. "Been nice talking to you, Judy." He barged past her, only to bump into Larry the moment he left photocopy room.

If he were walking any faster, he would have ended up on his ass; Larry was such a solid obstacle, no getting past him. "There ya are, Jake. Been looking for ya, buddy," the big man stated, clapping his meaty hand across Jake's back, the sting of it making him wince.

"Yeah, here I am."

It was then Tachibana came into view from behind the towering mass of muscle that was Larry. Jake's stomach twisted and ice ran through his veins. He was even more of a wreck now than earlier.

"Tachibana!" he wheezed, clasping onto the paperwork as if it would protect him from whatever followed.

He expected the worst.

Instead of receiving a punch to the face, Tachibana stated matter-of-factly, "I think we need to talk. Don't you, Jake?"

Jake's sweating. He looks petrified, the poor boy—I can't blame him. A good thing Riyu isn't at work, Tachibana thought. *Then again, where is he, then? He hadn't even called in sick from what I'd been told. That's not like him at all.*

Tachibana, Jake, and Larry were at the local coffee shop, *The Veranda Café*, to talk privately, Jake taking his break to do so.

Mister Anderson wasn't happy he'd taken one so early, but ultimately understood, Larry's presence the clear motivator, obviously.

No sooner had they settled, steaming cappuccinos in front of them, bottled water for Larry, when Jake blurted, "I'm…I'm so, so sorry, Tachibana. I truly am for what I did."

"What's done is done." Tachibana stared at Jake for a moment. A long moment. "But as it turns out, it's a good thing you did what you did," he added once the silence between them had stretched long enough, almost to being uncomfortable.

"Why's that?" Jake asked, eyebrow cocked, still on edge.

"You dodged a bullet."

Jake's eyes misted, his hands trembling as he held his cup. "You…you didn't, though. Did you?"

"No," Tachibana admitted. "And the wounds of it will live with me forever."

Jake hung his head. "I'm sorry."

Tachibana managed a small smile through the painful memory of what had happened. "Apology accepted." And with that he drained his cup and moved to get up. He'd made his peace. Said what needed to be said to the boy.

Jake leant over to catch Tachibana by his shoulder.

"He…he said he was going to kill me for not giving myself to him. Kill me, Tachibana!" The boy looked even worse than earlier, the look of sheer terror in his blue, blue eyes.

Tachibana, feeling for him, understanding, sat back down, the sting of doing so coursing through him. He winced, hissed through his teeth. "Riyu only ever wants complete control, and your disobedience would have rubbed him the wrong way."

"I get that." Jake wiped his eyes. "But what do I do, Tachibana? You know Riyu. What *can* I do?"

Seems I don't know Riyu at all, do I? Tachibana snorted, almost derisively, more to himself really. "I don't know—let the cops know what he tried to do, I suppose." He shrugged, genuinely at a loss.

Jake looked shocked. "No way that's happening. Cops hate queers like us. And they don't give a shit 'bout us either. Sure, they'll pretend they do, but they don't, and you know it."

He's right. And by the time anything does happen, Riyu could have done his worst. Perhaps even follow through with his threat and, heaven forbid, kill Jake. I wouldn't put it past him. Not now. Tachibana sucked in a breath, worry stabbing at his insides. *I got off lightly then, didn't I?*

Larry finally spoke, "Then we go find the fucker and tell him to back right off or he'll face the consequences." He cracked his knuckles, the sound loud and almost frightening. "That's what we do."

Both Tachibana and Jake looked at the man.

That's if we can find him. "I don't know where he'd be," Tachibana admitted, "because he's always either at work or at home. I mean, his brother who sometimes visits is in another state at the moment, so he won't be at his place. And he doesn't have any friends, none that I know of, anyway." *I should have realized his lack of friends is a red flag, shouldn't I?*

Larry suggested, "We check out the gentlemen's clubs on the strip one by one." He grinned. "A guy who's frustrated like how he must be feelin' 'cause he didn't get any ass when expectin' it, usually goes to one of 'em."

Tachibana felt uneasy, a flush of embarrassment. "If you're right, Larry, it seems Riyu punishing and then having his way with me wasn't enough to satisfy him either."

Larry narrowed his eyes. "The asswipe."

Jake interjected, "Then…um, seeing as we're going there, I want to go visit my dad. He's been worried about how you'd take all this, Tachibana. And he needs to know we're both cool with each other. We *are* cool, right?"

"We're good, yes." But now it was Tachibana's turn to be surprised. "But you say your dad's worried about me?"

Jake managed a quivering smile, a knowing one perhaps, but offered nothing to clarify his expression.

What does his look mean? Did Michael tell him something? Something about me! How he feels…about me? Tachibana didn't know how to react to that thought, so he dismissed it. *It's probably nothing, me just being oversensitive, reading too much into things after what happened.*

But before he could ask, Larry stood, chair scraping against the floor, blocking the sunlight moments later, and clapped his hands. "There are five gentlemen's clubs on the strip, so our work's cut out for us, lads. So let's go."

"I can't imagine he'd go to *Badda-Bings*," Tachibana said, *leaving four clubs to search.*

Larry grinned wickedly. "Not if he knows what's good for him."

Michael paced his office. If he was still a smoker, he'd have sucked down a packet by now, all because Larry was bringing Tachibana and Jake to see him. *Tachibana.* Beautiful, gentle, Tachibana. He began to sweat, palms and all.

I'm like a teenage boy thirsting over his first crush. God... *calm yourself, Michael. Calm yourself.*

"Are you sure he's alright to leave work?" Michael had asked on the phone earlier, thinking about it at least distracting him. For now. "I don't want him getting into trouble—more than he already is, anyway."

Nah, boss, Larry had replied with his usual finesse and directness. *Didn't take too much to convince his manager to give Jake some personal leave.*

"Alright, I'll see you soon, then."

Sure thing, boss. See ya in thirty.

Thirty minutes came and went, all too slowly and all too fast at the same time. Michael had checked himself in the mirror too many times to count, dusting off imaginary lint from his jacket often. Checked his breath even more, and hair.

I'm such a mess, he thought as the intercom buzzed and David's efficient voice blurted, "Larry, Jake, and Tachibana are here to see you, sir."

Michael needed a moment to still his racing heart. "Let them in, please, David," he said after clearing his throat, steeling his resolve.

"Yes, sir."

Larry entered first, as always. He went straight to the couch, taking a seat without asking. Michael didn't mind. He and Larry had a special understanding.

"Dad!" Jake called once he was revealed behind Larry's bulk, coming towards him.

Michael opened his arms to his son. "Are you okay?"

The result wasn't like in the movies, all coming up roses after their earlier reconciliation, but Jake did give him a quick, somewhat tentative embrace in return. It was something. Sure, they still had a long way to go between them, but progress was progress.

"Yeah, I'm fine." Jake quickly pulled away.

"Good to hear."

Jake offered a one-sided smile. "Getting concerned about me are you, Dad?"

"Believe it or not, I always have been."

"Okay..." Jake shrugged. "Whatever."

Yeah, it'll take time.

Although, before Michael could add anything more, attempt—probably lamely—to mend more of the broken bridge between him and his son, Tachibana cleared his throat.

He said, "I didn't think I'd be visiting you again so soon, Michael."

Michael, trying to lighten the mood after failing with Jake, replied, "And this time you've kept your clothes on."

But he knew his humor fell flat the moment the words escaped his mouth.

Larry rolled his eyes and groaned. Jake stared wide-eyed at him, mouth dropping open. Tachibana didn't look impressed.

That went down like a lead balloon, didn't it?

Michael, a flush of embarrassment coursing through him, gulped, feeling the weight off all their stares. "Anyway, moving on. What's the plan, fellas?"

Larry stood. "We search the clubs. And when we find him, we'll tell him to back the fuck off and leave Jake-y alone. Put the wind up him. That's what we do, boss."

Jake, glancing between Tachibana and Michael, a faint smile held on his lips, offered, "I suppose I'll go with Larry while he checks the club across the street."

Now concerned, forgetting his previous feelings, Michael immediately blurted, "You're not going inside it— you're not eighteen yet, remember."

Now it was Jake's turn to roll his eyes. "You don't have to keep reminding me, Dad. And no, I won't go inside. I'll wait in reception where I'll be watched on CCTV. I'll be alright. Okay?"

Michael, despite reservations, was happy with that. "Okay, then."

Another smile. "Thanks, Dad."

And there was another step of progress.

When Larry and Jake left, Michael turned to Tachibana. "We don't have to go anywhere if you don't want to. You don't owe him anything."

Tachibana, raw honesty in his voice, replied, "Despite

what you think about what happened, and even though I'm no longer Riyu's submissive and it's over between us, I know I've got to find him."

"I understand. But that doesn't mean y—"

"What business is it of yours what I do?" Tachibana spat, pain flashing in his eyes. "If nothing else, I deserve an explanation from him. Shouldn't that be enough?"

"I…" Michael stood open-mouthed for a moment, as Jake had done earlier. Without thinking, he grabbed Tachibana's arm, more out of instinct but also, perhaps deep down, because he *had* feelings for the young man. Feelings that perhaps needed to be revealed. "Please, just think about things for a minute. He hasn't treated you right, so you really don't owe him anything. And besides, I'm worried about you. Shouldn't *that* be enough?"

"Let go of me."

Michael didn't let go. "Give me one good reason why I shouldn't be worried about you?"

"Why are you worried about me? You don't even know me other than what you saw through your camera's lens last night."

"I care about you, that's what I know." Michael's heart pounded against the back of his ribs. He felt lightheaded. And it was Tachibana who did it to him.

But Tachibana scoffed. "Do people who care for others film them while they're having sex with strangers? Is that how they behave?"

"What are you trying to say to me?"

Tachibana yanked himself out of Michael's hold,

breathing hard. "You don't care about me, only how many hits your website will get because I performed for you."

"You're wrong. I *do* care about you."

"Prove it," Tachibana snapped, but his voice held something other than repugnance, his expression softening as well.

Does he feel the same as I do?

But Michael took the change as a subtle sign. Within a flash, unbelieving he'd done it himself, he grabbed Tachibana again, pushing him gently against the wall. Another split second later, and after a moment of pause where their eyes met, sensing the connection, the consent, he crashed his lips against Tachibana's, the result of a growing fever he hadn't felt for a long time compelling him to do so.

Michael moaned deep from his throat, a hunger he'd felt since first laying his eyes on Tachibana becoming satiated. And as their kiss deepened, moans from Tachibana as well, little shudders too, acceptance most of all, Michael's universe was born again.

He's...kissing me! And...and I think I like it...

Tachibana let himself melt under Michael's attention for a moment, let himself fall into the man's arms, be taken away. But while they held each other, kissed, tongues touching, shivers of pleasure tingling all through him, knees weakening, lightheaded, Michael's hands wandered down to the small of Tachibana's back, then to his buttocks.

The memories came flooding back.

Tachibana jumped, tearing himself away from their kiss, saliva dripping. At the same time, he also pushed on Michael's chest, the distance created between their closeness now seemed unsurmountable to cross because of how he suddenly felt. What he was reminded of.

What does he really want from me? Tachibana looked into Michael's eyes, his steel greys, trying to work him out, what he wanted, but found it difficult for the first time in a long time. It wasn't like Michael had dominated him or told him what to do either. Tachibana was at a loss. Felt like a fish out of water, to be honest. *But I now realize I don't want to be anyone's submissive anymore. And if that's what Michael wants, then it's over before it's begun.*

Michael looked bewildered, almost hurt.

But I do owe him an explanation. With a shudder of breath, the pain of what had happened searing through him, and the reality of it, Tachibana whispered, "I...I don't want you touching me there—it hurts me."

Something changed in Michael's expression. "What did Riyu do to you?" He held Tachibana's hands, gently, reassuringly, those eyes of his softened as much as the rest of him.

"He...he hit me..." Tachibana gulped, swallowed his pride. "Riyu hit me with a cane over and over until I bled, and when I collapsed and was crying from the pain he'd inflicted, unable to move and begging him to stop, that's when he kept going. He was possessed." His eyes stung with his emotions and the memory. He blinked rapidly. His chest tightened. "And that's...that's when he had his way with me. When he…fucked me, then told me he didn't want to see me again."

"Oh, god!" Michael's eyes went watery as well. "I'm so sorry this has happened to you. I don't know what else to say."

Tachibana lost control. Hot, searing tears dripped large drops from his eyes to roll down his cheeks in streams. He was shuddering, bringing his head into Michael's chest, holding him tightly.

He was held back.

"He hit me. He hit me…" He repeated over and over, crying, letting it all out while Michael comforted him.

Tachibana was held for an eternity.

The reception room of *The Pink Cockerel* was gaudy, too flashy for Jake's liking. *Who slaps cheap gold paint on everything*, he thought. Not classy at all. Not like *Badda-Bings*. No way.

No sooner had he ordered a coffee and sat down, watching Larry enter the *'You must be 18 or over beyond this point: ID checked'* area behind a shimmering golden curtain, a handsome young man sat in the empty chair next to Jake, beaming a leering smile.

"Hey, cutie, how are you?" he asked without delay, placing a warm hand on Jake's knee. "I'm Diego."

"And I'm seventeen," was Jake's flat reply.

The hand was removed immediately. Diego's face had also changed, even if he was obviously doing his best to hide his shock and disappointment at the same time.

"Oh, look, what'dya know, my friend needs me." Diego stood, pretend waving at someone in the distance. "Coming, Steve-o! Coming, mate." And with that he disappeared beyond that flashy but trashy golden curtain.

Jake chuckled to himself while he sipped his coffee. At least this tasted alright, unlike the rest of the place and its patrons.

This club really is a dive. Big time.

Before he even reached the bottom of the mug, Larry returned, which was a blessing. Two other guys had tried to hit on Jake, a third lining up.

"Thank god you're back," Jake blurted, standing, hugging Larry seconds later—his arms, even at full stretch, unable to get around the bulk of the man fully.

Larry pushed Jake away gently. "Riyu's not been here," he stated, not standing on ceremony. Not until he added, "Say, why are ya so happy to see me, buddy?"

"No reason." Jake giggled. "But I've gotta say, you do smell nice. What's the cologne you're wearing?"

"It's a combination," Larry replied enigmatically, winking.

"A combination?"

"Yeah, a combination."

Jake didn't press the matter. Clearly it was Larry's secret. He was fine with that. "Just to warn you, after I've turned eighteen, I'm gonna be all over you like a rash."

Larry chuckled, heading for the door. "When you turn eighteen, then we can talk."

"That's not a 'no' then, is it?"

"It's not a yes either."

Jake picked up his pace so he could walk by Larry's side, enjoying being in his protective shadow. "Just admit it, you like me."

"I admit nothing, buddy. Nothing." Larry glanced at him, smiling, something that warmed his massive face. "And stop thinkin' with ya dick again—I don't think I need to remind ya what happened the last time ya did."

"Hey, I'm a horny teenager." Jake laughed. "It's not *my* fault."

Larry then said the most surprising thing, warming Jake's heart and igniting hope within it. "But when ya are eighteen, no one'll treat you as good as me. Just so ya get that."

Jake swallowed, hard. "I-I don't…doubt it." And yes, because of Larry, his gentleness, his protectiveness, and his affection, there was a stirring where it mattered.

A big stirring.

Unfortunately, Jake didn't get much of a chance to relieve himself and his building tension in the nearest bathroom, public or otherwise. Larry was all business right now; he was paid on Jake's dad's time, after all.

They checked all the other clubs on the strip one by one. Three of them were nice establishments, one of which was equal to his dad's place in taste and style, although one club at the end of the strip was worse than *The Pink Cockerel*. It was nestled between a pawnshop and adult store, the kind of adult store with those infamous 'private' viewing booths inside, complete with sticky floors and used condom décor. Gross.

Jake couldn't believe the place was open; it was that

tacky. Then again, going on the clientele he saw entering while waiting for Larry, rough looking bikers, rougher looking drug dealers, and pumped-up pimps, he then understood why.

Each club served a purpose, he supposed.

Unfortunately, Riyu hadn't been in any of them.

"What do we do now?" Jake asked, slapping his hands against his sides, exhausted and disheartened by the lack of results from their investigation once they were outside in the fresh air again.

Which was just as well because only moments before, Larry arrived to save the day...again, some fat hairy bear of a biker who stank of stale BO and staler beer had taken an interest in Jake, making goo-goo eyes at him.

Jake shuddered, still did.

"I dunno."

Larry looked equally perplexed as he led Jake away from *that* club, enjoying he was once more in the mountain's shadow where he felt safe.

"Honest answer, hey?" Jake asked, able to breathe easily again.

"Always."

Jake sighed, feeling defeated now, but in a way glad he hadn't confronted Riyu. "Then I suppose we go back and see my dad."

"I s'pose we do."

Tachibana was a little better after he'd had a good cry. "I feel so embarrassed I did that." *Really embarrassed.*

"You've got nothing to be ashamed of. Nothing." Michael offered another tissue. "And besides, you've got good reason to cry."

Tachibana took it graciously, even though wiping his nose with it, complete with snorting sounds, was anything but gracious. "What's your story, then?"

Michael looked taken aback. "What do you mean?"

"You know what I mean."

"Ah…our kiss."

"No. I liked that. What I'm referring to is what your intentions are. Because before we can go on from here, I need to tell you something."

"Fair enough." Michael sat on his office's couch, leather creaking, looking both concerned and gentle, as always. "Then let's talk."

Tachibana joined him but did so in such a manner he was once more sitting sideways. The pain was still real. All of it.

"I need to tell you that…that I'm not going to be anyone's submissive anymore. I don't think I can even… bottom anymore either. It's too…painful. Not the act of it, because I used to love that, but…but the memories it stirs up. They're too much." More tears then fell.

Michael leant over, holding Tachibana, both of his hands. "I understand."

"Let me finish, please." Michael nodded; Tachibana added, "I want to be loved. Simply loved. But I don't know how to go about it because…because I've always been told what to do when it comes to such things. I don't want to be told anymore either. I want to feel it. Feel it how it should be felt. Do you understand that?"

"Trust me, I do."

Tachibana looked up through his misty eyes, once more giving Michael his full attention. "That's why I asked you what your story was. I can tell you've been through a lot. More than me, I'd say."

"I have—but you've already met my biggest mistake and joy."

"Jake."

"Yeah, him."

"What happened?"

Michael shifted his weight. "Long story short, I treated his mother like she was nothing all through our relationship, one where I tried to convince myself I wasn't gay and failed miserably. I took my frustrations and anger out on her. Because yeah, I had plenty of it." He paused, deep in thought, his eyes once more going watery.

He continued, "I got drunk one night, got her pregnant, and now it's taken me seventeen years to get Jake to even talk to me. In a way, what happened with Riyu broke the ice between us." He snorted a laugh that held no humor. "And even though it's not what I would have wanted, not at all, Jake can at least stay in the same room as me without us screaming blue murder at each other…"

I can hear the pain in his words, even after all this time. Is that how it's going to be for me? "You acted like Riyu…a selfish jerk."

"I did. And as a result, for years Jake used me as his

personal ATM machine to punish me, only visiting when he wanted money. I can't blame him for that. I can't."

"We all have ghosts that haunt us."

"We sure do."

"But Jake seems okay now, right?"

Michael nodded. "He is—I think he's realized I'm not the monster he thought I was."

Tachibana had to ask, "Do you talk to his mother?"

A snort of disdain. "No chance. She wouldn't talk to me for all the money in the world—she hates gays, you see."

"Jake's gay, isn't he?"

"Yeah, and I think him realising it has been a big part of our reconciliation too."

"That's a good thing, then." But Tachibana needed to refocus the conversation. "Tell me...are you a top or bottom, or both?"

"Wow!" Michael laughed. "Forward, aren't you?"

"I have my reasons."

"Yeah, you're wondering that if I'm a top, how are things going to work between us, am I right?"

"Something like that." *How does a top be with a guy who doesn't want to bottom? Who...can't bottom?*

"Let me first tell you, love isn't about sticking it in a hole. And if it's love you want, I'm your man, Tachibana, because, as you've no doubt already worked out, I need love as well."

He is like me. He kept on track by saying, "Also, and even though I appreciate what you did when choosing gentle guys for me for *The Interview* I insisted I take part in because of my naivety...my stupidity, there'll be no more filming of anything when it comes to what we do together. Okay?"

"Whatever you want, I want as well."

"Thank you." Tachibana felt himself warm all over. "Will you go with me to Riyu's apartment so I can collect my things, please?"

Michael kissed Tachibana on his cheek, taking his tears away with his touch. "Sure thing—but where are you going to stay after that?"

"At a friend's place." Tachibana smiled. He was glad Judy from work had offered to put him up on her couch until he could find something better. Despite her quirks, he liked Judy. "And no, I've already arranged it, so don't try and change my mind."

"I wouldn't dream of it. What you do, the decisions you make, I respect them all without question or condition. I respect and care for you above all else. Have done so since I first saw you. So please don't ever think otherwise."

"Is that part of this love thing?"

"It sure is."

They kissed again, that time softly, breathtakingly, and oh so wonderfully. Tachibana couldn't help liking the feeling of being kissed, touched, and held with so much intent it hurt him in a better way. Helped heal his damaged soul, even if the scars remained. He returned Michael's intent with as much affection.

I could get used to this.

When parted, Tachibana, through trembling lips still tingling from the affection he'd received, uttered, "I take it we're boyfriends or something now, right? Because I'm sure you don't kiss all the guys you meet like that."

Michael laughed; Tachibana loved the sound of it. Laughter had been rare between him and Riyu.

"If you want us to be," he said, "then that's what we are."

"I think I do."

And yes, after the disaster that was Riyu, Michael might just be the one. But time will tell. Time will tell.

With lots of bangs and clatters coming from the kitchen, Judy was cooking something involving red sauce and pasta but wasn't spaghetti bolognaise, which piqued Tachibana's curiosity.

A curiosity that was only satisfied when she served it up.

"Here, hun, get this down ya gob. It's me mum's recipe, and I always cook it to cheer folks up." She placed a massive steaming plate full of lasagne in front of him, smelling divine.

Judy lived in an inner-city apartment, as Riyu did. Her place was a lot smaller than his was, though. It was basically four rooms: a bedroom, kitchen, bathroom/toilet, and lounge. He'd managed to sit at her petite dining room table located at the end of the lounge room's two-seater couch without too much bother from his buttocks.

I think this means the medicinal cream is finally *working.* The thought was almost a relief. *Then again, perhaps I've just mastered the art of sitting in such a way I'm avoiding contact on my sorer parts.*

His back would probably suffer later.

"That Riyu is such a bastard," Judy declared, sitting with Tachibana and tucking into her meal moments later, the masticating sounds of her food loud and irksome, just like how she chewed gum.

"He is," was all he could offer, concentrating on anything but her eating.

"Did ya know, he was seen hanging around one of the local high schools. Rumor has it, he were tryin' to pick up boys to fuck in exchange for weed."

"Err...what?"

She shrugged. "That's what I were told."

Tachibana couldn't believe it...or perhaps he could. Riyu had gone mad. Worse than that, he'd become an even bigger pervert than he already was.

What a creep. Tachibana shivered uncomfortably. "He never showed signs of wanting underage boys before. Not until Jake...you know."

"My man, how could ya not have known?" Her eyes widened, as if in shock, red sauce dripping down the front of her to disappear into her cleavage—an ample one considering she was only wearing an oversized T-shirt and not much else.

Seemed Judy was already comfortable sharing her place with a gay man. More so when she reached in with her napkin to wipe it away. She then threw the red sauce-stained napkin onto the table next to her plate, eating again as if nothing happened, chewing loudly.

Tachibana averted his eyes, feeling warmth grow in his cheeks, embarrassed for her. Not that she was embarrassed, he was certain. He supposed he didn't want her to catch him staring. Not that he was. It's just that he'd never shared a meal with a woman before, especially dinner, and he was unsure of what to do. He felt...awkward.

Normally Riyu told him how he should act, what he should eat, and how he should do it.

Judy didn't care one way or the other.

About anything.

He found he liked her company. *She's a good friend, for sure.*

But before Tachibana could answer her because he went deep into thought, like always, she added, "Riyu cracks onto any boy, no matter how old they are. Any boy who'll give him the time of day, anyway. He's a pedo, no doubt. Why'd ya not see that, Tachi?"

He didn't mind she shortened his name either. "I was too busy doing the things he demanded of me, I suppose."

"You poor baby."

She pointed her lasagne-filled fork at him. "I bet he got ya to shave everywhere so you looked younger than ya are, am I right?"

Tachibana flushed even more heat. "Um...something like that."

"The dirty bastard."

But Tachibana wanted to get back to the matter at hand, take the attention off him. "What high school was Riyu seen at, do you know?"

She shrugged again. "I think it were one of the local ones, Preston High. Yeah, Preston High."

"How'd you know this, Judy?"

She winked. "Pfft, gay guys think they've corn'ed the market on givin' blowjobs to get what they want outta men, don't they? If ya gotta know, I sucked off a cop mate, and he sings like a canary 'fore he dumps his load down me throat. An' if I swallow it, he buys me shit too. Win, win, hey?"

"Is this cop your *boyfriend*?"

She smiled knowingly, wickedly even. "One of 'em, yeah—but he's in the lead, for sure."

I've truly got to admire Judy. I really do. And because of her, seeing as I now know the cops are investigating Riyu and what he's up to, he's obviously on the run—he hasn't been back to his apartment. Tachibana smiled. *He deserves everything coming to him, and I'm going to make sure he gets it too.*

"Can I ask what made you go to your cop friend to find this out, Judy?"

"Sure, hun." She mopped up her plate with garlic bread, shoving that in her mouth. Around her food, she continued, "When Riyu didn't call in sick today and ya told me he wasn't home, I got real suspicious knowin' him like I do. So I then talked to Jake-y. That little cutie pie told me Riyu weren't at any of the clubs either. Weren't anywhere he looked. So yeah, I called Hank, me cop friend I blew, to see if he'd heard anythin'. He told me what I just told ya. Easy as that."

"You're the best, Judy. Truly, you are."

"I know I am." She stood, dusting crumbs off her T-shirt-come-nightdress, it was that big fitting and loose. "And 'cause I cooked, ya can clean up and do the dishes."

"No problem." *After I've done that, I'll call Michael and tell him about this.*

Jake took another personal day off work; he had to work Saturdays sometimes. Mister Anderson understood…well, Larry helped a lot with that. And most times Jake found he could only smile at Larry, the man was that amazing.

So today, and after he'd spoken to his dad earlier, found out he'd gotten information from Tachibana who got it from Judy, they had a lead, as slim as it was, to try and find Riyu.

They'd start with where they knew he'd been.

"There it is on the right." Jake pointed.

Larry pulled the car into the Preston High's carpark. The main building, red-bricked and with heritage white-framed windows, loomed.

When Larry killed the engine, he said, "Good a place as any to start, I reckon."

Jake felt concerned all of a sudden. "Can we just go in there and ask about Riyu? Are we allowed to do that?"

Larry turned to look at him, eyes glinting. "Ya don't know this, Jake, but I'm a jack of many trades. When I'm not workin' for ya dad, I'm not only a registered private investigator—which is why I *can* go and ask questions, to answer ya—I'm also a massage therapist as well."

Jake only heard two words out of all that. "You're a massage therapist?"

Larry burst into laughter. "Somehow I knew ya would focus on that. And no, I work some weekends at the local footy club…so it ain't what ya think."

Jake felt himself blush. "Even so, I have the sudden urge to play footy now."

"I bet ya do." Larry got out of the car, coming around to open Jake's door for him. "But how 'bout ya stop thinkin' with ya dick for a minute so that we can get on with findin' Riyu, hey?"

Jake felt even more warmth, that time all through him. "I am who I am."

"Good thing too, huh." Larry patted him on his back as Jake got out of the car.

"Yeah, good thing." Jake, despite everything, could really fall for Larry. Really fall for him, hard. And that wasn't his hormones talking. Larry, despite being a mountain of muscles, was soft, kind-hearted, and cared, and that was so sexy it made Jake's head spin, it really did.

Together they headed towards the principal's office.

Much to Jake's disappointment, the principal of the school couldn't offer anything more than, "Why yes indeed, the man you've described was caught by the sport's shed offering drugs to our boys in exchange for sexual favors yesterday. I phoned the police immediately. Most distressing for all of us it happened. Most distressing."

"I take it the guy ran soon as he were found out, right?" Larry offered.

"Indeed, he did. And I hope he's caught. I really do."

"That's our plan," Jake chimed in.

From there, they checked all the local high schools,

sporting clubs, and anywhere else they thought Riyu might have made himself known. All of them were places teenage boys hung out.

Jake felt sick thinking about that.

Tachibana was right, I really did dodge a bullet, didn't I?

The rest of the day they didn't see hide nor hair of Riyu. They'd failed, although Jake didn't think of it like that. He'd spent it with Larry. And to him, that was a good thing. A very good thing.

After dropping him home, Jake said hi to his mum and stepdad then headed for the shower. Suffice it to say, the thought of Larry massaging him, rubbing oil all over his nakedness, made the water even hotter than it already was. It was a long shower.

Before Larry drove off, he'd said, "Tomorrow we'll start checking the primary schools."

Jake gasped in shock. "You think he'll go after boys *that* young?"

"Wouldn't put it past the fucker."

"Then…I'll see you tomorrow."

"Not if I see ya first." A laugh, a wink, and a smile that melted Jake's heart to fill his shoes with gooey goodness followed before Larry pulled off the driveway.

Jake stood stock still, heart fluttering, watching until not even the car's taillights could be seen within the growing darkness. *Yep…there's no doubt about it. I could so love him…*

Part Four

The weeks passed.

Tachibana's physical wounds had healed, but the soft skin of his buttocks was left scarred. To him, terribly scarred. They looked ugly. He hated them so much.

It's a permanent reminder of how stupid I'd been—I can't even look at them. His stomach turned. *I don't want to either.*

As such, the scars he felt in his mind remained as well. More so. The only consolation was that he had Michael. His boyfriend had been so supportive since he'd left Riyu that fateful day.

Michael was always there for him when Tachibana needed it.

To listen.

To comfort him.

To accept him, even when his moods fell into darkness.

Tachibana, unbelievably even to himself, was beginning to understand what it was to be someone's equal. What it was like to have someone appreciate him for simply being himself, not demand anything of him. Sure, old habits were hard to break, Tachibana often correcting himself, but as each brick was slowly taken away from the wall of his past that'd once surrounded him, he also began to understand something else.

He began to understand what love was.

"How are you today?" Michael asked, handing Tachibana their now traditional morning cup of coffee, a strong espresso with a couple of tea biscuits placed onto the saucer—the sweet to the bitter.

"Same as always, I think." But he smiled, feeling it to his heart as he studied Michael, thinking how things had changed for the better.

Michael kissed Tachibana on his forehead; he liked that. "Better than being worse."

He'd been staying at Michael's apartment more and more lately, practically lived there now. Not only was his boyfriend's place massive, he had a spare room. And as much as Tachibana appreciated Judy, loved her as a good friend, sleeping on her tiny couch wore thin very quickly. His spine would never be the same, and he'd developed a crook in his neck even Larry's massage skills couldn't work out.

"Any word from Larry or Jake?" Tachibana wanted to know something, anything, about where Riyu could be.

Tachibana never forgot what that man did to him, even when he slept. The nightmares often too real. To keep him on edge, the disgusting creep hadn't been seen since the report of him doing what he did at Preston High all those weeks ago.

Riyu hadn't been seen at his apartment—Tachibana knew that because Judy's cop friend Hank had told her they were monitoring the place. The rent hadn't been paid for the past month either. As such, from what he was told, by the end of the week the sheriff's office had been given the clearance to place all of Riyu's belongings into storage and re-rent the apartment.

"No luck, I'm afraid," Michael said, bringing Tachibana to the moment. "It seems Riyu's gone to ground."

"I hope they find him soon." *Knowing he's still out there is stressing me out.*

"They will." Michael kissed Tachibana upon his lips that time. A shiver of delight ran through him. "Worms like him always crawl out from the woodwork eventually, especially when they're not satisfied."

"I feel sorry for whoever he chooses to take his frustrations out on."

"So do I."

Michael's continuing kisses stirred something within Tachibana; something that'd been brewing for a while. At the same time, he couldn't quantify it. He'd never experienced it before.

Is this what it feels like to be loved by someone? Truly loved?

Tachibana wanted to make sure.

Reaching to pull Michael into him, breathe him in, touch the exposed skin of him, his neck and stubbled chin, with his lips hungrily, Tachibana soon crashed his mouth onto his boyfriend's. He opened it for him, his sudden excitement making him pant, needing Michael to deepen what they already shared.

A moan, a shudder, delightful tingles; Michael returned Tachibana's intention equally.

He's really into me, as I'm really into him.

For the longest time, eternity and back really, they kissed and kissed, jaw aching, lips numb, and heart beating so fast it sent Tachibana's head into a wonderful spin. Made his dick harden too.

This feels…so good.

When finally parted, breathless, wonderfully so, Michael, still caressing Tachibana, whispered, "You seem different."

Without delay Tachibana replied, "It's you who's changing me."

"For the better, I hope."

Tachibana breathed out, one that came deep from his soul. "My grandmother once told me to never chase after the boys who give you butterflies because it's a feeling that can never be repeated. But I think she's wrong." He smiled, planting more kisses on Michael's warm, wet lips. "You give me butterflies all the time. So yes, I think I'm changing for the better. And that's all because of how you've treated me."

Michael stared for a moment, eyes misting. "As an equal."

"Yes, as an equal."

From that moment on, Michael knew Tachibana was the one.

The man he'd marry.

The man he'd care for, always.

The man he'd grow old with.

Then, one lazy Saturday afternoon a few days later, the time mostly spent in Tachibana's arms, Michael caressing his back and hair lovingly, plenty of long deep kisses and affectionate looks between them, his boyfriend's phone rang unexpectedly, startling him. His ring tone was a nightmare, so loud and cheesy—like an '80s dance tune, it was that bad.

Michael couldn't help but laugh.

Tachibana fished the phone from out of his front pocket, but not before Michael playfully blocked him from doing so, wanting to keep touching him. That was until Tachibana smacked his hand away, giggling as he did so.

"You're no fun," he stated, sticking out his tongue.

Tachibana held his laughter. "It's Judy, so I've got to answer it." He put it on speaker. "Hello, Judy. What can I do for you?"

She replied, "Hank wants to see ya and Michael as soon as ya can get to the cop shop. He's got some news for ya both."

Tachibana suddenly drained white; Michael held him with more intent, comforting him. "Riyu?" he asked nervously.

"Yep, I reckon so."

"Then tell Hank we'll be there as soon as we can be."

A giggle. "Don't rush, lads. Hank's on his break, and I'm 'bout to thank him for bein' a good boy, yet again."

"Swallowing this time?" Michael interjected, rather cheekily he admitted.

Tachibana glared at him; Judy didn't skip a beat, though. "Hell yeah, mama needs a new dress."

More laughter, that time shared by them all.

"Okay. We'll be there in an hour or so," Tachibana said. "Does that sound alright to you?"

But she'd hung up.

Michael, shrugging even if smiling, offered, "Seems to me Hank's truncheon suddenly became more important than talking to you."

"You're so wicked," Tachibana said, now tickling Michael where he was the most ticklish, under his armpits.

He knows all my weaknesses, him being the biggest one of them all!

Because, and as Michael roared with laughter, loving that he did so as they both rolled around on the couch, embracing, kissing again and again, he realized Tachibana was laughing with him.

It was good to hear his unbridled laughter.

Things are slowly changing for him. And even though we haven't consummated our love yet, what does it matter? But when the time does come, when he's ready, I'll have something special for him. Something he'll love, I know it.

When Tachibana had finished, both of them panting, even sweating a little because they'd laughed so much, their physical play wrestling the cause, Michael realized he felt so much in love, achingly so, that he didn't want to go anywhere.

Then again, in this case, he knew he had to.

Michael asked, "How are you feeling…after Judy's call, I mean?"

"If it gives me some closure, then I know I'll be better."

"I tend to agree."

An hour or so later, they were standing inside the busy police station—the 'cop shop' as Judy called it—where

Hank worked from, waiting for the man; his break obviously not over yet.

Michael found that amusing.

"I'm sure he won't be long, chaps," one of the other officers said, distracted by numerous other people all vying for his attention. "Take a seat if you want to."

As they sat and waited as instructed within a sort of waiting area complete with wilted potted plants that'd seen better days, Michael felt the urge to reach out and hold Tachibana's hand.

He stopped himself.

Because, and of course, while within one of the largest bastions of toxic masculinity, he decided against it. Michael simply didn't like cops at the best of times; the sentiment no doubt returned, as most cops he'd met hated him.

Hated gays, more specifically.

The bastards were always visiting his club, trying to catch him out on any little detail to either fine him or try and close the place down. *Just because* Badda-Bings *is the best, it attracts the wrong kind of attention sometimes.*

While waiting he received a call from David, all business related, of course.

The young man was as efficient as always.

After finishing with the rundown of the mundane day-to-day stuff, David asked, *I've got a few of our regular guys asking when* The Interview *is happening next. What do I tell them, sir?*

"It can happen whenever you organize it, David. Just line up the right bottom with the right tops. You know what to do. I trust you. Oh, and you can film it as well. I won't be doing that anymore." He glanced at Tachibana.

His boyfriend smiled.

Err...okay. Sure thing, sir, David said.

"Are you alright with that?"

I am, sir. Thank you for trusting me with this, I know it's been your project for so long. I won't let you down.

"I know you won't."

David then paused. Michael could tell there was more, obviously not business related at all. "What's the matter?"

Umm, oh nothing, sir. It's just that Jake is here to see you.

"Tell him I'll be there as soo—"

Dad! Jake interrupted, obviously snatching the phone away from David. *I've got something to tell you and I can't wait.*

Michael was surprised, but then he grinned. *It's great he trusts me enough to tell me things now.* And that realisation caught him off-guard a little, made him choke back his emotions. "What...what is it...son?"

I'm in love!

Again, astonishment. "Anyone I know?"

Larry, Dad! I'm in love with that big, beautiful hunk of a man named Larry! Isn't that great?

Michael smiled from ear to ear. "I couldn't be happier for you; Larry's a great guy and I know he'll look after you... well, he'd better!" Michael laughed.

I know it too. The excitement in Jake's voice was clear. *And when I turn eighteen next month, just so you know, I want to have a huge party at* Badda-Bings. *Oh, and after that you're*

*paying for a fancy hotel room for me and Larry, because he's
gonna be my first!*

"I'm paying for all that, am I?"

Yep, you sure are.

Michael realized he couldn't be happier. He had
Tachibana by his side, and now he had one very happy son
who'd confided in him, even if he still wanted money like it
was an endless supply. Michael smiled, though. Things
were smelling like roses. Finally. "Well, okay then. And I'm
glad you're happy."

Me too. Talk to you soon, Dad.

"Yes, we'll talk soon—I love you." Tachibana glanced
at Michael after he'd spoken those words; in response he
whispered, "It's Jake I'm talking to now, not David."

"Ah." A raise of understanding eyebrows from
Tachibana, a smile added.

Yeah, bye. Jake hung up.

Okay sure, there was no return 'I love you' but for
Michael, more than enough progress had been made.
Before he could ruminate over the conversation—because it
did make him feel good—a massive uniformed man came
up to them, all moustache and bulging biceps stretching his
shirt.

"Let me guess, you must be Hank?" Michael offered
without even needing to read the cop's name badge.

"That I am." He glanced between the two of them.
"Come with me, gentlemen. You'll want to see this before
we do anything else."

• • •

Tachibana and Michael were led by Hank to an interview room beyond the main welcome area of the station. Surprisingly, it led into another room, one that had that one-way viewing glass, just like those CSI crime shows did.

I didn't think these were real, Tachibana thought.

But the fact the glass was there wasn't what mattered; the view it offered did. Because inside the room sat Riyu, shoulders slumped and looking despondent, and looking sorry for himself.

Tachibana took in a sharp breath, his heart pounding hard against the back of his ribs. Michael held him around his shoulders, pulling him close, clearly sensing his distress. Because yes, Tachibana *was* stressed.

So much so, he was glad Michael was holding him; his knees had almost given out on him already. He felt faint confronted with Riyu, for sure, more than he thought he would be.

Even though I'm no longer with him, he can still affect me so much, it's terrible; it really is.

Tachibana began to sweat, feel breathless as his chest tightened. It was incredible.

Hank, interrupting Tachibana's spiralling in time to snap him out of it a little—thankfully—stated, "We caught him a couple of hours ago at one of the local primary schools." The man snorted his clear disgust. "Riyu allegedly tried to abduct a boy playing basketball with his friends after he chased an errant ball. Good thing a few older kids caught the creep and called us."

Michael gasped. "A *primary* school?"

Hank replied, "Yep, the one next to Preston High."

But Tachibana wanted to know more. "How old was the boy, officer?"

"Hey, call me Hank, Tachibana," the man said, nice and friendly. "It's not like I don't know you, is it? I mean, Judy doesn't stop yapping on about how great it was that when you lived with her you didn't try anything funny. She really likes you—guess I do too, even if it's by association."

"Even though he's gay, you mean, don't you?" Michael said, still holding Tachibana.

Hank shrugged. "Makes no difference to me if he's gay, straight, or whatever. A friend of Judy's is a friend of mine, no matter who they love, am I right?"

I think I like Hank. He seems quite liberal...for a policeman.

But clearly the conversation had gone off the rails, so Tachibana brought it back by repeating, "How *old* was the boy, Hank?"

Hank sighed. "Nine. The poor kid's nine years old—he's undergoing counselling as we speak. His parents are beside themselves too." A pause as a pained look crossed his face. "We don't know for sure, but we believe Riyu sexually assaulted him before his friends realized that he was gone too long and went to help him."

Tachibana felt the room spin.

Again, thank God Michael was holding him.

Then, and not surprisingly, Tachibana held Michael, feeling his tears flow as he found himself cradled within his boyfriend's chest where he felt the safest, where he felt loved.

My nightmare may be over for the most part, but that poor

nine-year-old boy, he'll live with whatever happened to him for the rest of his life.

A long moment of contemplative and reflective silence followed, one where Tachibana's mind worked overtime. He had a lot to think about; but out of all of it, he realized one thing. He had to do something to ensure Riyu wouldn't hurt anyone else ever again.

He had an idea.

As such, it was Tachibana who finally broke the shocked quiet that'd blanketed them with its gloom.

Wiping his eyes, doing his best to compose himself, he said, "To help with things, to make sure he doesn't hurt anyone else, I want to lay formal charges against Riyu for what he did to me. I can show you the evidence of it too."

Hank's eyebrows rose. "Are you sure that's what you want to do, Tachibana?"

"It is." Tachibana glared at Riyu through the one-way glass, hating him even more.

More than he'd hated anyone in his life.

A snort full of scorn came from Hank. "Good on you, because with what he got caught for, and with your charges added to the ones the boy's parents will no doubt file, I'd say Riyu won't see the light of day for a long time. He won't even get bail; any judge will deem him a menace to society without even a blink of an eye."

"Good," Tachibana spat. "He deserves nothing less than to rot in jail as far as I'm concerned. And I hope he does."

Michael chimed in, "I can also talk to Jake, my seventeen-year-old son. I'll bet you a cocktail at my club that he'll want to say his piece about what Riyu tried to do to him as well once I tell him all about this; and with your support, of course, Hank."

Hank smiled. "We'd be interested to hear that, for sure. Nothing better than seeing a monster get what's coming to him. Nothing at all."

Tachibana said, "Where do I go to do what I have to?"

Hank gestured up the hallway to the main area of the station. "Follow me."

"Before I go, can I say something to Riyu?" Tachibana added.

Hank nodded. "If you must. But I'll go in with you. Protocols and all, you know."

"Fine with me." Determination came over Tachibana. "I won't be long, anyway."

"Do you want me to come with you?" Michael asked.

"I do."

Together, all three entered the interrogation room. As soon as they were inside proper, Riyu looked up. There was defeat in his eyes. Tachibana realized he looked pathetic.

I can't believe I used to love him.

Before Riyu could speak, even utter a word, one that begged, spoken in anger or otherwise, Tachibana said softly, "You might think that being your submissive made me weak, Riyu. But I'm here to tell you, it didn't. It didn't. It has made me stronger."

He took in a breath, having said all that in one go.

"I want to tell you," he continued, "that because of what you did to me, you broke me. But from the ashes of my destruction by your hand, a great phoenix was born. I am now that phoenix, and you, you're nothing to me now."

More breaths, his heart racing.

"Remember my words when you're all alone, your ass bleeding from being fucked so hard, frightened by shadows, and scared of raised voices because the other inmates you'll be forced to live with treat paedophiles with contempt. You deserve it."

Tachibana felt giddy, drunk on the euphoria he felt because he was finally standing up for himself. Michael, his support, comfort, and growing joy, moved to hold his hand. Tachibana took it. He liked that he did without hesitation, more so because it was not only done in front of Hank, but Riyu as well.

Riyu obviously noticed—the look of jealousy unmistakable.

The hate too.

Tachibana wasn't done, though. "Remember what I gave you, Riyu, and how you didn't appreciate what I did for you. Not one bit." He scoffed. "I hope I never see you again for as long as I live, because these words will be the last ones I want to waste on someone like you."

Tachibana, without waiting for a reply, not even saying goodbye either, turned and walked out of the interview room, Michael still holding onto him. He was really sweating now, everything numb, but he'd done it.

He'd said what he needed to say to get his closure.

Now the healing can begin.

When well clear of the interview room, heading back

to the main area, Michael squeezing Tachibana's hand, asked, "Do you want to talk about it?"

Tachibana looked at him, breathing better now. "I do." He nodded, adding a small smile. "Because now that it's finally over, I can."

"Then, let's talk."

Tachibana came close, so close his lips ghosted across Michael's. "But can we talk after we're out of here?"

"Of course."

"There's one more thing, though."

"What's that?"

"I want us to be together tonight."

"Together?"

Tachibana's smile widened, one full and filling him with joy, the first time he'd done so in a long time. "Yes, together, *together*, if you know what I mean."

"Oh, I do." Michael's cheeks flushed red, but his loving stare didn't leave Tachibana.

"I'm glad you do."

Back at Michael's apartment, Tachibana, always feeling a whirlwind of emotions, more so lately, now felt nervous. He wasn't sure how to proceed now he'd agreed to be with Michael in a more intimate way.

Now they were going to be close, as close as two people can be.

What am I supposed to do if I'm not being told? Do I let him lead? Do I? What?

But to his relief, Michael didn't rush. Didn't do anything other than give plenty of kisses and deep and warm embraces for ages as they rolled around on the bed.

Also, and equally slowly, they took off each other's clothing. When Tachibana was naked, aroused as much as Michael, that's when things came into stark focus for him. He felt exposed. But not because of what he wanted to do, but because, for the first time, someone else would see his scars besides himself.

As Michael moved, kissing him all over, Tachibana blurted, "Don't look at me so closely, please." He felt shame wash through him after verbalising his fear.

A fear he'd never had before, it almost overwhelmed him.

"What's the matter?"

"My...my scars," he said weakly, almost inaudibly.

Michael embraced Tachibana with more intent. "Your scars are a reminder of your strength, not your weakness."

"They're...ugly."

"No, they're not." Michael then did the most astonishing thing; something that amazed him, he had to admit. He moved so he could kiss the marks marring Tachibana's buttocks one by one, tenderly and warmly and with so much love, his breath was taken from him. "They're beautiful, just like you."

Tachibana felt himself shudder before he began to cry, his throat tight, heart racing. "Is this...is this how 1-love feels?"

"I don't know. How do you feel?" More kisses, longer lasting and even more sensual and tender.

"Like I'm the only one who matters to you despite how scarred I am, physically and mentally."

"Then yes, that's how love feels."

Tachibana turned to face Michael, nervous, suddenly shuddering with his emotions, all of them at once, and hiccupping. "Then…hold me, and let's learn how we can consummate our love together, please."

"Before we do, I've got something to tell you."

Another kind of fear suddenly stabbed at Tachibana's aching-with-love heart. "What? What have I done? Don't you want this?"

"I so do." Michael kissed his tears away, like he always did. "And stop thinking the worst. You don't have to do that with me, not ever. No. What I wanted to say was that for you, because you mean so much to me, because I care for you in so many ways, I want to bottom for you."

Tachibana gasped. "I beg your…what?"

Michael gave even more passionate kisses. "I've never felt like this with anyone before, only you, Tachibana. Be my man. Make love to me so I can feel it deep within me. I need you."

"Oh god, I…need you so much as well."

More nerves found him, but soon the heat of what they shared, their electricity, their passion, eased them a little. Without even knowing it, his mind a wonderful muddle, Tachibana found himself on top of Michael.

Looking down at him, a strange position to be in, right into his steel greys, admiring his gentle face, was something that took his breath away. He felt his vision go misty again. This time, he loved it.

He's so handsome.

Michael began moving underneath Tachibana, an act that caused their skin on skin contact to heighten how he felt. More so when their erections, now hard, Tachibana's especially, leaking so much he knew, were pressed and rubbed together. He shuddered. His breaths became even more shortened.

I could just stay like this forever, me feeling him, him feeling me. It's amazing being naked in someone's arms. Amazing.

But Tachibana felt a spark within him. One that had started small but now grew into a fire. He did want Michael. Wanted him how they both wanted it.

"Put it in me, Tachibana," Michael whispered between kisses, kisses that were deep and passionate and fuelling the fire within Tachibana even more. "I can't hold out much longer."

Michael opened his legs for Tachibana, the lust on his expression clear. He should know, Tachibana felt it himself. Michael also leant over and took a small bottle of lube from off the bedside table, handing it to him.

"I don't know how good I'll be at this," he said, taking the bottle.

"Love can't be judged, so however you express it or however long it takes, even if it's quick or awkward, it'll be wonderful because it's from you."

Tachibana's stomach flipped. That was new. He loved it. *I'm really going to do this. I'm going to top the man I have fallen so hard for in such a short time. I can't believe it.*

After applying the lube liberally, Tachibana shuffled into position. After pulling back his foreskin, more lube applied, also to Michael, he pressed his hardness where it mattered.

Tachibana knew from experience how Michael felt the

moment before the 'pop' of entry. The man moaned, a little shudder, a hiss. Tachibana's stomach flipped even more as he pushed gently with his hips, the sensation strange but intoxicating at the same time.

"Oh god, yes!" Michael said, grabbing the sheets, quivering, eyes shut tight but holding a smile.

An erotic smile.

Tachibana couldn't describe how he felt when his hardness, all of it, right to his manscaped pubes, suddenly went inside Michael like it was sucked in when he pushed harder. He panicked at first, unable to quantify the experience of having someone's anus clenching around his dick. So warm. So tight. He shuddered, feeling it to his balls.

At that, he let out a sharp breath, moaning.

I'm really doing this!

Tachibana, still kneeling, let himself remain inside Michael, not doing anything, not moving, but simply enjoying the weird sensations of being there.

He became overwhelmed, more than at any other time he'd felt. As such, his tears fell from those misty eyes of his in large drops.

"You look...happy," Michael said, opening his eyes, tear-filled as well.

"I am."

"So am I."

"But I'm also...I can't explain it, but I love how a part of me is inside a part of you, if that makes sense."

"It does." Michael opened his arms. "It's the connection

we've both desired. Now, come hold me while you make love to me. I need you to bring me to climax."

Tachibana didn't need to be told twice. He was good at that. Within moments, he'd collapsed onto Michael, kissing him, holding him, letting their connection intensify. And intensify it did.

Because, before too long, he gained a sort of staccato rhythm. Not a great rhythm, probably not even good either, but considering this was his first time, to Tachibana it was fantastic.

What made it more so was the fact Michael writhed underneath him uncontrollably, really causing his dick to seat itself within him. They really were one.

And as he felt himself build up to the inevitable release, so quick, Tachibana no longer thought of them as being two people. And that surprised him.

I mean, after all, I've only got my dick inside him. How can such a thing make me feel as though I'm a part of him too? That we're connected by more than our parts somehow?

Tachibana moaned, keeping his kiss tight to Michael's lips, their tongues as intimate as they were with each other.

This is truly heaven.

Michael began caressing Tachibana's back, thankfully—and not like before when they first kissed—his contact never went lower. Tachibana didn't want his buttocks caressed, his scars touched again, not yet, because that would break the spell they'd been weaving together, he knew it.

Breaking their kiss, he whispered, "Thank you."

"With me, you will always be safe and cared for. I won't

promise it either, because promises can and do get broken. No, I'm just going to do it. Care for you by what I do for you. That much you must know."

"I do." *I really do.*

And for whatever reason, mostly because it had been building up to this point, tears still falling, happy ones, Tachibana felt himself release at a much deeper level. A release that was more profound, more cathartic than when he cried. He let go more than he had ever let go of himself before.

And he gave it all to Michael who could now hold it for him.

"Oh…ah!" Tachibana came and came, with it went all the tension that'd been built up for far too long, way before he'd even met Michael.

Never to be seen again.

It was unbelievable.

He collapsed into Michael's arms, crying, heaving, shoulders shuddering, but loving it. Loving it so much he only felt complete comfort.

Another strange feeling.

Underneath him, Michael shuddered too. He'd come. Tachibana could feel the warmth of it against his stomach.

They kissed and kissed.

The connection salted by their tears and glued by Michael's ejaculate. Tachibana didn't want to let him go. Not ever.

They stayed like that for many eternities.

Time passed slowly.

Evening turned to full dark.

But their moment wasn't done.

Tachibana, remaining inside Michael, still aroused, kissed his heated, salted lips, little sparks of joy emanating from that simple but profound touch now that it had been fuelled by so much more than anything he'd felt before.

Because he was finally free.

He said, "It's you and me from now on, isn't it?"

"It is," Michael replied.

"Then, can I make love to you again, please? I love doing it with you. I also love the love you give me in return, because out of everything I've been through, it's our love that heals me the most and make me feel appreciated."

"You are more than appreciated. And I can't think of anything else I'd rather do but have you in my arms."

"Me either."

"I do love you, Tachibana Kushano. I love you with all my heart."

"I love you too, Michael Brock." A deeper kiss, even more affectionate. "Not just with my heart, but with everything I am, because I understand now what it is to give love and feel love in return. Thank you."

"Thank you too."

The End

Author's Note

The title of this story refers to someone not appreciating what they have, just as a cat wouldn't appreciate being given coins (in Japanese folklore). Which, in Riyu's case, this is clear. He didn't appreciate Tachibana, even when Tachibana did all he could for him. For that, Riyu paid the ultimate price.

About the Author

By day I'm a humble physical therapist...and by day I'm also a writer of sweet & saucy boyslove stories (18+). I sleep at night as an old fart like me should. I'm both self-published and traditionally published. Other than that, I live with my partner and two cats and live my best life.

Website: http://konblackeboyslovewriter.com

Twitter: http://www.twitter.com/blackekon

Also by Kon Blacke
Published by Dreamsphere Books

Immortal Whispers
Kon Blacke

The Whispering Monks have foretold change to the world, and it's fast approaching. They also speak of the mortals who'll be involved.

Hereward, a lord knight who only worships the steel at his side, as the mad magician Ealdræd has taken away everyone he had ever loved. Wymond, an oblate determined to find his true self, even if it means turning away from everything he has ever known. Beornræd, a powerful magician who fears to love again after the cruelties of his past. Kieron, a stable hand with dragon blood flowing through his veins and is the rightful heir to a realm of unimaginable beauty.

All four will travel their own paths, to destroy their pasts and rebuild their future, as they thwart the evil plans of Ealdræd and his conduit, the immortal Abbot Hosho.

The whisperings continue through epic battles, both on the ground and in the sky.

The whisperings shall continue beyond the aftermath.

As it has been foretold.

More from Deep Desires Press

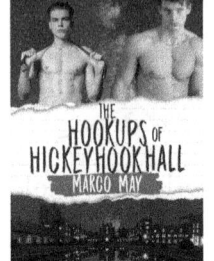

The Hookups of Hickeyhook Hall
Marco May

Jenner is gay and has a crush on Michael. Unbeknownst to him, Michael is bi and has a crush on him in return. But there's one huge obstacle in the way of professing his love. Their parents just got married to each other. Now, they're officially stepbrothers.

Both young men are determined to move on and leave their feelings behind, and what better way to do that than to dive into the challenges of starting a new life at Hickeyhook College? Their new lives are full of quirky roommates and stupid rules...and the discovery of an underground sex club with both students and staff that offers students the opportunity to cheat their way through to graduation without all the stresses of normal college life. With both young men in the club, it brings Jenner and Michael dangerously close, making it impossible to ignore the feelings they both swore to leave behind.

As sticky as their new situation is, it's about to get stickier. The powerful Dean Wicket sees the emerging relationship between Jenner and Michael and he's determined to get in the way...because he wants Michael to himself.

When the truth of Jenner and Michael comes out and the world is against them, these two men must fight with all they have to hold onto true love.